He wasn't expecting a visitor.

Outside the elegant library of his spacious home he paused briefly, noticing the woman standing before a painting of his mother and father over the large sofa where he'd fallen asleep the night before. There was something vaguely familiar about her. He recognized something in the way she stood.

As if sensing his presence, she turned slowly, and his heart stopped.

Carla stood before him, an uncertain look marring her lovely features.

"From your expression, I'm sure that I'm the last person you expected to see, Shayne," she said. Her sarcasm did not fail to reach him.

For a moment she stood still and silent.

Then, like a scene from a daytime soap opera, Carla, the woman who haunted his dreams, crumpled to the floor....

WAYNE JORDAN

lives on the beautiful tropical island of Barbados, where he's a high school teacher who writes romance. Since joining the ranks of those who are published, he's had people constantly asking him why he writes romance. The answer is simple. Writing romance seems as natural to him as breathing. Not that he started out wanting to be a romance author. He initially had dreams of being the next great Caribbean writer, and then he discovered popular fiction and found himself transported to strange but exciting worlds that he longed to visit. Since he was a voracious reader, he read books from every genre, but romance became the genre that best allowed him to escape the crazy world we live in. He writes to make people "laugh and cry and laugh again," and if he succeeds in doing this, he knows he's done a good job.

one gentle
KNIGHT

WAYNE JORDAN

KIMANI
ROMANCE

 KIMANI PRESS™

ISBN-13: 978-0-373-86027-2
ISBN-10:   0-373-86027-7

ONE GENTLE KNIGHT

www.kimanipress.com

Printed in U.S.A.

Dear Reader,

I hope you enjoy Shayne and Carla's story. When I conceptualized THE KNIGHT FAMILY trilogy, I wanted to do two things: I wanted to write a series of stories in which one of the main characters was truly Barbadian and not an American visiting the island. I also wanted to write more stories set in my beautiful island, Barbados.

In *One Gentle Knight*, Shayne and Carla find love despite their shaky beginning. Both of them needed to leave their cynicism about life and relationships behind. They needed to heal and embrace the wonder of romance and love. By the time you read this letter, book two, *To Love a Knight*, scheduled for release in late 2007, will be in my editor's hands, and I'll be busy at work on the final book of the trilogy, *Always a Knight*.

In my last letter, I promised you the third book in my Buchanan Brothers series, but when I finished *Embracing the Moonlight*, I knew I wasn't ready to write Daniel's story. I wanted to give him time to grieve. Just a few days ago, Daniel's story came to me in that quiet time early in the morning when my characters talk to me. As soon as this trilogy is done, I'll be working on his story, *Chasing Rainbows*.

I'd like to thank all my readers for your wonderful support, and I wish that you continue to enjoy the stories I write. Visit me at author@waynejordan.com or www.waynejordan.com.

Blessings,

Wayne J

To Cheryl Brathwaite—colleague and friend.

This story is a tribute to those mothers, like you, who know the joy of watching their tiny bundles grow to be strong, healthy individuals. Sharing your knowledge of the emotional roller coaster of taking care of not one but two preemies has only made this story a better one.

To Renee Thomas—colleague and friend.
Thanks for proofing this manuscript.
Of course, you get to read this story long before everyone else.

To my Literature students in 4–1, as I promised, this one is for you.

Prologue

Shayne stood naked by the window, but the crisp chill of the morning air didn't bother him.

It never did.

In fact, the morning ritual provided him the opportunity to forget the stress and problems of the day before and formulate plans for the busy day ahead. For a few precious moments each day he felt at peace and at one with nature.

However, this morning, he did not embrace the familiar sounds. Instead, he felt an acute feeling of loneliness.

On a normal day, he would hear the sweet melody of the steelpan his brother, Russell, insisted on playing each morning. Eventually, the baby of the family, Tamara, would add her off-key soprano to the mix.

Somehow, he'd grown to love the strange morning music. The sounds represented all that was good in his life, his family. He'd thought that would be enough to make him happy, so he'd settled comfortably into the dual role of provider and protector.

But today was no normal day.

All that had changed yesterday. After eight years of being father, mother, brother and friend to the two most important people in his life, he was all alone.

Of course, Gladys still remained constant. She'd taken her place within the family, but the plantation house would not be the same without his brother and sister. They were his life.

Shayne moved away from the window, his gaze immediately falling on a photo of Tamara and Russell, which hung on the wall above his bed. He smiled, trying to ignore the sharp ache in his chest. Both sides of his family had been blessed with good looks. Shayne had their father's angular features, but Russell and Tamara were the truly attractive ones. They shared the perfect blend of their mother's and father's heritages.

No one, however, could fail to see the similarities between him and his siblings. They each possessed the same quirky smile that lit up the black, often unreadable, pools of their eyes and the stubborn tilt of the Knight chin when they couldn't get their own way.

Sometimes Shayne wondered about his part in carrying on the Knight dynasty. He had no desire to get married, so it was unlikely there would be any children from him. And Russell was so caught up in his studies that Shayne wasn't sure what would happen there. Maybe someday he'd have to ignore his personal feelings and do his duty. For now, he preferred not to dwell on the subject.

Glancing down at his watch, Shayne quickly slipped into gray track pants and a white tank top and left his room. He had several business meetings today and wanted to be sure to meet with his foreman.

At the end of the corridor, he turned toward Russell's room.

Halfway there, he stopped abruptly.

His brother was not here. Russell was in New York and Tamara was in Jamaica. Both were about to begin postgraduate degrees.

He was finally alone.

And he didn't like it one bit.

For that reason, Shayne knew he needed downtime before he went crazy. He wanted to get away before he left for England for six weeks on business. That moment, he decided to accept an invitation he'd received to spend a week at the recently opened Hilton Hotel. He owned shares in the company that had built the hotel and had received an invitation to spend a complimentary week there. Maybe he could finally relax, have some fun and, most important, enjoy life.

As he was about to call the hotel, a quietly grumbling stomach reminded him he had not eaten since returning from the airport to see Tamara off the evening before.

He hoped that Gladys had put the coffee on.

When he reached the kitchen, the sharp aroma of his favorite Blue Mountain blend greeted him. A brief note stuck to the refrigerator informed him that Gladys had gone into Bridgetown. He smiled, knowing not to expect the housekeeper back anytime soon. Gladys loved to shop and made sure she spent a full morning in the city each week.

Sitting at the counter, Shayne quickly filled his mug, savoring the experience, before he picked up the phone nearby and punched in the hotel's number. When the receptionist answered, he wasted no time in making his reservation.

"This is Shayne Knight, one of the hotel's shareholders. I'm calling about the invitation I received. I'll arrive on Monday and will be staying for the whole week."

The pleasant female voice thanked him for calling and informed him that a suite would be available. Business conducted, he put the phone down and headed back to his bedroom. His meeting with his foreman, Patrick, was in less than an hour and he hated to be late.

At least, however, he'd taken a step in the right direction. He would go to the hotel, meet a beautiful woman with ample breasts and spend the week making passionate love to her.

Yeah, sure.

Knowing the person he'd become in the past few years, that was unlikely to happen. He'd probably end up sleeping all week and aching to return home.

But just maybe, he'd be lucky. He wasn't looking for anything much. Just a week of harmless fun.

And definitely…

…no strings attached.

Gladys watched as Shayne's car drove down the driveway, turned on to the road and disappeared. She was worried about him and hoped that this time away from the plantation would help him to deal with the loneliness she knew must be driving him crazy.

She loved him as if he were her own son. She'd

watched him grow into a tall, handsome man, a man any mother would be proud of.

When his parents had passed away about ten years ago, he'd been forced to leave his wild life-style behind. Shayne had loved to party. Despite his love for revelry, he'd always been a straight-A student in high school. With a brilliant mind and an aptitude for science, he'd entered university to pursue a degree in agriculture, all part of his grooming to take his father's place. Fortunately, Shayne's love for the land equaled his father's and he'd spent every free minute learning every facet of the plantation's operations.

But both his wild life and his studies had come to an end with the sudden and unexpected deaths of his parents.

Shayne had surprised Gladys with his maturity. He'd withdrawn from school and taken on the responsibility of running one of the largest sugar plantations on the island and succeeded. He'd turned his brilliant mind to wringing a profit from his family's sugar business, and, now, at thirty-two, he was one of the most powerful landowners in Barbados.

What had impressed Gladys most, however, was the ease with which he'd taken on the role of father and mother to his younger brother and sister, Russell and Tamara. At twelve years old, the twins had been devastated by their parents' deaths.

For a while, Shayne had buried himself in the rum that flowed freely in the bars around the island, until one morning, he'd come downstairs and told her he was going off to meet with Patrick, the plantation's foreman.

After that day, Shayne had taken on the responsibility of running the plantation and caring for his brother and sister.

But Gladys was worried. Shayne needed a woman. Yes, he needed a wife, but for now she'd settle for a woman to give him some good "Bajan" loving. She was not impressed by any of the uppity women who vied for his affection, and, thank goodness, neither was Shayne.

Of course, she knew he had the occasional brief liaison, but she wanted so much more for him. She wanted him to find a good woman…and, most of all, love.

Until he found those things, she knew he'd never be truly happy.

Chapter 1

Paradise.

She was in paradise. Carla Nevins never ceased to be amazed by the beauty of Barbados. Her best friend, Sandra, had frequently told her about the island, but it was only after making her first trip to the island several years ago that Carla had finally understood what Sandra'd meant when she'd said after her trips that she'd been to heaven and back.

Barbados was surely heaven on earth.

In the distance, the Atlantic beckoned, its frisky waves crashing onto the beach. The sun's rays, no longer the blistering white of the day, were now a clear gold that gently caressed and warmed her.

The first signs of dusk and the tropical sunset that she found awesome, were already making themselves evident with the palest of oranges and yellows splashed lightly across the sky. She'd spent most of her day down on the beach, and knew it was time to take a shower and prepare for the long restless night ahead. Since she'd arrived on the island, she'd partied every night into the wee hours of the morning. The guests and locals who frequented the nightclub at the hotel were a wild and friendly bunch. Like them, she had totally immersed herself in the rhythm of Barbados' nightlife.

She didn't mind losing herself in the island's pulsating rhythm. As a matter of fact, she preferred it that way. Anything to block out the nightmares that still haunted her. Now, on the island, when she collapsed on the bed in the early hours of the morning, she was too tired to dream. Her memories seemed at rest…at least, for the time being.

Carla lifted the book on her lap and, for the umpteenth time, reread the first paragraph. Frustrated, she put it back. This paper fantasy wasn't what she wanted or needed. She wanted to see him again. The man she'd seen at the reception last night.

The man whose image now remained etched in her mind.

Squeals of delight from children in the water interrupted her musings. Again, her eyes skimmed the beach, wondering if he'd ever appear. She slowly looked to the left, then to the right and then doubled back to the bar just beyond the tennis courts.

It was *him*.

He stood there, looking as bored and indifferent as he had the night before. He looked in her direction, and their eyes met, touched and lingered. Although she was a distance away, she knew what she'd seen in his eyes.

The same smothering awareness she'd seen the night before.

She was reminded of a performance she'd seen of Shakespeare's *Romeo and Juliet*. In that moment, when the two protagonists become aware of each other across the crowded ballroom, they experience something profoundly magical.

Last night, when she'd seen the handsome stranger for the first time, she'd felt the magic. All night, there'd been this acute awareness, as if they both knew that the path destiny would take was inevitable. She'd been glad that she'd gone to the party.

When she'd read one of the colorful announcements that hung like Christmas decorations all around the grounds, she'd been tempted. The party with its promised local dishes and, of course, the famous lethal rum she'd heard several of the guests talk so much about, had beckoned her. So, last night, Carla had stood sipping her glass of rum punch and wondering why she was suddenly feeling strangely light-headed and surprisingly happy.

And then he'd walked in…and her heart had stopped.

He was tall and muscular and also quite handsome. Not in the classic way, but a rugged, sunkissed way.

And he oozed sex appeal.

Pulse-pounding sex appeal.

Carla saw it in the way he carried himself, the way his broad shoulders swayed when he swaggered and in his intense gaze.

She'd watched him for the whole night, her eyes devouring every inch of him. And she knew he was just as aware of her. Yet, neither of them had made the first move.

She wanted him.

In the early hours of the morning, back in her room, she'd lain in bed alone, her body betraying her, as she'd ached for a man she didn't even know.

She'd imagined him naked, his strong arms wrapped around her waist. She'd placed the pillow between her legs, hoping to stem the ache that had slowly but sweetly reminded her that she was still a woman. It had been so long.

Richard had come to mind, as vivid and clear as he often had in the years since his death, and, for a moment, she'd, once again, felt the overwhelming grief that always seemed to consume her, threatening to take her to the brink of madness.

Carla would never forget the accident that had taken her husband, Richard, and their unborn child from her. She'd been seven months pregnant when Richard died. And, when she'd held her stillborn daughter in her arms, she'd cried because she knew her last physical link with her husband was also dead. She'd wanted to die with them. At night, when the dreams came, she still did.

She closed her eyes, wanting to remember the feel of Richard's hands on her body. Despair filled her when she realized that his presence and his touch were fading.

She opened her eyes.

The man was gone.

Carla had hoped that he would come in her direction. Maybe she should have made the first move. She'd probably missed out on her chance to have…

Sex!

That was what she needed.

Her best friend, Sandra, had told her that much. "What you need, girl, is some hot-dirty, scream-out-loud sex. Maybe you'd start to live again," she'd said.

And Carla was already coming alive, thanks to her mystery man. Who was he and where was he?

Suddenly, her body tingled and the rush of warmth to the core of her womanhood forced her to lean forward.

He was back.

Half naked.

He wasn't wearing the skimpy trunks that most of the tourists sported, preferring the loose boxers the local boys and men wore and a sheer cotton shirt.

She was disappointed. She'd wanted to see the evidence of his manhood, that telltale bulge that a woman's eyes always noticed.

In her dream last night, she'd imagined what he would look like. Long, thick and firm. Yes, long. She knew he'd be long. Knew, because in her wildest dream, she'd felt the thick length of him as he'd entered her slowly. For some reason, she knew that what she'd dreamed would become a reality.

She knew he would come to her.

And, as if hearing her, he started to walk toward her.

Shayne had to find out why the woman from the party last night kept staring at him. Not that he had a serious problem with her. Actually, he couldn't help staring at her, either. As a matter of fact, the way she'd looked at him last night had given rise to a randy need he hadn't experienced since his teenage years.

He wanted sex.

Needed sex.

He started to walk toward her. More than any-thing, he wanted to touch her. He needed to feel a willing, ripe body that he knew would respond to his. He wanted to bury himself between the supple legs of a woman who wanted uncomplicated sex just as much as he did.

He wanted a woman to help him to live again; something he hadn't done since his parents' death. He'd spent the past ten years working around the clock and making sure his younger brother and sis-ter had the love and attention they needed. He'd put his life on hold to make them happy.

He hesitated, drawing to a halt. What he was about to do almost made him turn around and head back to his hotel room. Then his gaze locked with hers, strengthening his resolve and he continued to-ward her.

Last night, he'd thought long and hard about what he was going to do and he had every inten-tion of completing his mission.

Shayne could feel her eyes on him as he drew closer to where she reclined in a beach chair, and he wondered how she'd respond to what he was about to propose. Would she reject him? Would she think he was crazy? Actually, he wouldn't blame her if she up and ran away. He thought he was acting recklessly, too, but there was something about her that made him think she felt the same attraction he did. He knew she had experienced that same powerful awareness last night. Her silent, heated response to him had been proof enough. For some reason, this woman had taken control of his mind and body.

Maybe he *was* a bit crazy.

In his dreams, he'd made love to her all night and, in the early hours of the morning, he'd awakened, his body covered in sweat and his manhood erect and straining for release.

Already, he could feel the familiar stirring, the sweet ache of anticipation.

When he reached her, she broke eye contact. Unaffected by the rebuff, he reached out to take her hand.

"Come with me." His boldness amazed him. He'd planned to introduce himself, first, invite her to dinner...and then seduce her.

The flash of energy that raced through him when she placed her hand in his was sudden and unexpected. His heart stopped and, for what seemed like forever, he lost himself in a pair of the most unusual pale-brown eyes he'd ever seen.

Damn, he wanted her.

"Come with me," he repeated.

He released her hand and waited until she rose

from the beach chair and slipped into her sandals. Then he turned and headed in the direction he'd come from. She fell in step beside him, her stride as urgent as his.

Minutes later, as the elevator moved upward, Shayne reached for her, his lips covering hers as he realized that he couldn't wait until they reached his room.

He needed her now.

He sipped of the sweetness she offered, her eager lips parting to accept his probing tongue. As he kissed her, his every sense seemed heightened. Her nipples pebbled against his chest, forcing a strangled groan from him.

She was so sexy, everything he'd imagined she'd be.

Instinctively, his left hand found one of her breasts. Left or right? It didn't matter. He groaned with satisfaction as his hand kneaded the already turgid point, and he felt its eager response.

In the midst of the haze that enfolded him, he heard the sharp ding of the elevator door as it opened.

Reluctantly, he pulled away from her, wanting to spare her the embarrassment of being caught making out in an elevator. No one entered, and, again, he reached for her hand as they stepped into the corridor.

As they entered his hotel room moments later, Shayne was conscious of the fact that what he was about to do was madness. But there was a strange rightness to what was happening between them. And he knew that this day would be forever special. He could hear his heart pounding, the tiny pulse at the curve of his jaw throbbing in time with the steady rhythm echoing throughout his body.

As the door closed behind him, he felt her hands on him, her touch firm, as she explored him, teasing every nerve in his body. His hands clenched at his sides, he placed his back against the door, letting her have her way. The door's coolness did little to stem the shimmering fire that raged uncontrollably inside.

When she reached to unbutton his shirt, he eased away from the door, helping her to take it off. Then her hands touched him again, moving across his chest until she sought the slight rise of his right nipple. She smiled, rolling it between her fingers and, then, like the whisper of the wind, her lips teased first the left, then the right nipple, before she placed it in her mouth. Like a baby, she suckled and then she stopped and a coolness lingered there. He opened his eyes, realizing that he had closed them.

He could wait no longer.

* * *

When he entered her for the first time, Carla bit her lips to contain her response, but her lips parted, her pleasure evident in the scream of joy that escaped her lips. It was as she'd imagined. His long thickness filled her until she could feel every throbbing inch of him.

Instinctively, she wrapped her legs around his waist, drawing him even closer. When he groaned, she realized that his arousal matched hers.

"Damn, woman, you were born for me. Being inside you feels so right," he moaned. "Move with me."

And then he started a slowly tantalizing movement, stimulating the core of her womanhood, until it took all her willpower not to spiral over the edge. His strokes, firm and controlled, caused every fiber in her body to tingle with awareness. In minutes, she felt the slow build of pressure and then the rush of pleasure as she shuddered with the power of her release.

For a moment, he stopped, breathing heavily. "Woman, you almost made me lose control. I don't want this to end so soon."

"No problem," she replied. "We have all night. I don't think once will be enough."

"Once will definitely not be enough," he whispered, his voice husky with desire, his mouth hovering over hers.

When he started to move again, his lips captured hers. This time, there was desperation in his movements. He stroked her hard and she reveled in the power of each thrust of his body. She joined him willingly, matching each stroke with her own. This time, his breathing was erratic, his movements less controlled, but she rode with the wave of desire.

Gripping his buttocks, Carla brought him closer, spurring him on, wanting him to join her this time. Her own release was near. With one final thrust that made her throw her head back and scream again, his body convulsed, as he moaned with the power of his orgasm. Seconds later, she joined him, her body shuddering with the intensity of her release.

Exhausted, she wrapped her arms around him, pleased when he did the same thing. Her head against his chest, she listened as his heartbeat slowed and his breathing became a soft whimper.

All she remembered thinking before she'd fallen asleep was that she'd been to heaven and she definitely wanted to go there again.

Shayne looked down at the naked woman sprawled on the bed before him. Damn, she was lovely, and he wanted to make love to her again. He glanced down at his penis, erect and ready, knowing that he'd make love to her again before the sun disappeared beneath the horizon.

There was a knock at the door and he quickly slipped his robe on before bending to pull the covers over Carla. Before he turned toward the door, she stirred, opened her eyes, and he saw the telltale flare of heat.

She wanted him, too.

He opened the door, taking the pizza box from the bellboy and gave him a handsome tip. Closing the door, he returned to the bed, placing the box on the nearby table.

"Want to eat on the balcony?" Shayne asked her.

She shook her head. "I'd prefer to stay here."

"My housekeeper, Gladys, would be appalled, but since she's not here and I'm not telling, the bed would be perfect."

Shayne quickly found two wineglasses, removed the bottle of pinot from the refrigerator and moved toward the bed.

He placed the glasses on a tray before placing the pizza box on the bed.

As he was about to sit on the bed, she raised a hand, stopping him. Her eyes shimmered with passion.

"You're going to have to take that dressing gown off. It wouldn't be fair for me to be naked while you're dressed."

Shayne hesitated, but slipped the robe from his shoulders and joined her on the bed.

"Your wish is my command," he said, nodding. "As long as you can handle the consequences of your request—or should I say, order."

"Oh, I'm sure I can handle anything that comes my way." Shayne heard the promise in the huskiness of her voice.

"I'm sure you can. However, let me propose a toast," he said, raising his glass toward hers. "To hours of hot, unending sex."

He heard her sharp intake of air. He was sure that, like himself, she was aroused, but he was enjoying this verbal foreplay.

There was no touching, just the spark of awareness between them. He felt the familiar stir of arousal, feeling a brief moment of embarrassment. Somehow, he felt exposed, vulnerable. He didn't even know her name. That fact only heightened his excitement.

While they drank wine and ate the pizza there was no need for words. The drumbeat of anticipation rang in his ears.

When Shayne finished the last piece of pizza in the box, he placed his wineglass on the floor.

Then he reached for Carla, drawing her to him. Shayne lowered her upper body to the bed, allowing the momentum to take him with her. He could feel her breast against his chest and ached to put the firm flesh between his lips.

He trailed his lips down her neck, nibbling as he journeyed south and then he paused, unable to keep his eyes off her.

When he pulled the first dusky nipple into his mouth, Carla groaned, a jarring sound that seem to come from deep within the core of her body.

Shayne sucked and tugged, enjoying the arching of her upper body as he moved against her.

Shifting his head, he took her other nipple into his month, honoring it with the same attention. Underneath him, Carla moaned, her volume increasing as she gave in to the passion burning between them.

For a while, he suckled, enjoying her soft sounds of pleasure. But then Shayne wanted to kiss her. He moved upward, delighted when her lips met his halfway.

His tongue slipped between her lips, tasting her, teasing her. He grew more excited with each passing moment.

When her thighs fell open, allowing him access, he knew he wanted more of her, more from her. He wanted to feel her warm tightness around him. He wanted to know her in the most intimate way, again. When her body jerked against him, his own tensed immediately and its response to her was as powerful as the first time they'd made love.

He could wait no longer.

Shayne raised himself slightly above her and then plunged inside her until he felt as if he'd jumped off a cliff and now soared above the clouds.

Carla's legs wrapped around him, drawing him in even farther, and he reveled in the heat coursing through his body.

Shayne stroked her lustily, allowing his penis to touch deep within her. The flames intensified as they moved together in the age-old dance of passion accompanied by the earthy music they made.

Too soon, he felt the fire inside flare as every muscle in his body came alive. Shayne didn't want it to end. He wanted to prolong the feeling of euphoria that only came with the ultimate climax.

Shayne felt Carla's body tense and he gave himself over to the joy as she joined him in flight.

He felt his every muscle and nerve tighten, and then he lost control and he shuddered with the intensity of his release.

When his eyes locked with hers, he saw a look of surprise and wonder wash over her face. In that moment, he knew that something strange and special had taken place between them.

Minutes later, he drew her to him, holding her gently against his chest.

When he closed his eyes, he wasn't aware of the tears that trickled down her cheek.

All he knew was that he wanted her again.

* * *

Carla stretched, sighing with utter contentment. Her body ached all over, but the weariness she felt only served to remind her of the incredible night spent with a stranger. He'd taken her to a place she'd never been to and, to be honest, she wouldn't mind going back there again.

She opened her eyes slowly, her vision adjusting to the dimly lit room. With the thick curtains drawn, only valiant trickles of sunlight succeeded in allowing her to see the naked man stretched out beside her. Hearing gentle snoring, she turned toward him and her breath stuck in her throat. Despite the dullness of the room, she could see every chiseled ounce of his body. He lay on his stomach, his arms tucked under his pillow. Her eyes trailed the wide expanse of his back to his narrow waist and down to his firm, sculptured behind.

When she realized the snoring had been replaced by heavy breathing, her gaze moved upward and immediately locked with his. His eyes, hot flames, blazed, reflecting the same desire she knew burned in hers.

She wanted him again.

As if he'd heard her, he rolled toward her, straddling her and parting her legs in the same fluid movement. When he entered her this time, her response didn't differ. She welcomed every inch of his thickness, amazed that somehow the temporary emptiness had disappeared. With each thrust, she raised her body to meet his, wanted to join in the dance performed by centuries of lovers. Carla realized that this moment would never be enough, that, somehow, this man had totally captured her body and she'd already lost a part of her soul to him. In her mind, words of love he would not want to hear tore from her lips, but she made sure that they remained there.

Then the sweet pounding in her head started, and the familiar soar of pressure sang in her ears. When the moment came, she didn't care that the walls of the room might not be thick enough. Her cries of release joined his and all she knew was that she'd met the man of her dreams.

Shayne jumped awake as something screamed in his head. Damn, his cell phone.

He slipped from the bed, trying not to wake the woman who lay next to him.

Finding his pants in the dimly lit room proved to be difficult, but he eventually found them and pulled his phone from the pocket. Recognizing the number, he quickly flipped it open.

"Patrick, there had better be a good reason for disturbing me," he said softly. He didn't want to wake his lover. She needed her rest. Two days of unending lovemaking must have taken their toll on her.

"Sorry to disturb you, Shayne, but there's a fire in the fields to the north of the plantation," Patrick said. "The fire service has already arrived. The two families who live along the road that borders that area have lost their homes."

"I'll be there in ten minutes."

"Shayne, take your time. The only way you can get here in ten minutes is if your car can fly."

"Fifteen," he responded with a chuckle. "I'll see you in a bit." He folded the phone.

This was definitely not how he wanted his week to end, but he had to go. The fire could spread and destroy some of the sugar crop.

Quickly putting his clothes on, he slipped into his sandals, all the while, watching the woman who lay asleep.

Damn, she was beautiful. Why did the fire have to happen at this time? Shayne didn't want to leave her, but he'd be back. He hoped this wouldn't take too long.

Before he left the room, he went over to where Carla slept.

Bending toward her, he touched her cheek with the gentlest of kisses.

God, she was incredible. Already, he was hard

again with his need for her. Somehow, he didn't think he'd tire of her, and that scared him.

But he'd be back.

He'd definitely be back.

The drive to the site of the fire took longer than he'd expected. The increasing traffic in Barbados remained one of the few things about the island that annoyed him. He loved to drive in the countryside, but going into Bridgetown was something he tried to avoid as much as possible.

At the Warrens roundabout, the car crept along inch by inch. Images of Carla were the only things keeping him from going crazy. She'd gotten under his skin and, for the briefest of moments, he questioned his no-strings-attached resolve.

But his few days with his woman were only a fantasy. In a day or two, he'd be back to reality. The passion, the lovemaking, the tender touches, all were parts of a dream he was currently living.

Now, he was going back to the real world.

Going back to the loneliness.

The thought made him sad, but holding on to a glimmer of a dream was foolishness.

For now, he'd enjoy the reality of the moment. And he had every intention of enjoying every minute with his lover.

Chapter 2

When Carla woke the next time, the dream had ended as quickly as it had begun. She was alone in bed.

Her eyes immediately went to the floor. His pants and shirt, tossed there in the heat of passion, were nowhere in sight.

He was gone.

Only memories bundled in rumpled sheets and the lingering musky scent of lovemaking remained. However, she didn't need to close her eyes to conjure an image of him. He remained fixed on the slate of her mind's eye.

Carla groaned.

Her body still ached for his touch. She wondered where he'd gone. In the two days since their meeting, they'd not left the hotel room. The hours of lovemaking had only been interrupted a few times to eat and sleep.

She'd hoped that in her final days on the island they would get to know each other. In their few moments of conversation, she'd only discovered his name and the fact that he owned a large plantation on the island. Beyond that, there was very little she knew about Shayne Knight.

During their lovemaking she'd sensed his loneliness and desperation. Despite his attempt to remain untouched by unexpected feelings and his effort to maintain an emotional distance, Carla realized that, like her, he was losing.

At moments when he believed her to be asleep, she'd felt the whisper of a kiss or the gentleness of a caress. Most of all, she could not fail to respond whenever he wrapped his arms around her and she embraced his sad emptiness. Her own emptiness could not help but respond.

Troubled, Carla slipped from the bed, allowing the sheet around her to fall to the floor. The chill of the air caressed her still-heated body and her nipples tightened. She reached for her robe and a sheet of paper floated to the floor. She hesitated, dreading the message she knew would be there.

Or maybe it was a note telling her he would be back.

Carla bent, slowly picked the note up and placed it on the bedside table. After her shower, she would read it, but now, she wanted to wash the lingering warmth from her body. She headed to the bathroom but turned abruptly.

She couldn't wait. She had to read the note now. She picked it up again, unfolded it, her hands trembling.

The message was simple.

Had a great time. Have to return home to deal with an emergency.
Shayne.

That was it?

No telephone number? No 'I'll see you later?'

Why was she disappointed? Isn't that what they'd agreed to?

No strings attached.

Yes, that had been the agreement. But somehow, she thought the time spent together had meant something. That somehow he'd been moved by the incredible lovemaking as much as she had been.

At first, what they'd taken part in had been sex as primitive and unemotional as two strangers might expect to experience. But something had happened as the clock slowly ticked the hours away. The feelings had changed; the kissing and touching had become more than physical manifestations.

Her soul had become involved.

Her heart had been touched.

Carla felt a profound melancholy. The fact that he'd left without knowing how to contact her meant that, unlike her, he was unwilling to reach out for more.

Despite the glimpse of forever, he'd walked away.

No strings attached.

Carla stepped in the shower and turned it on. The sharp sting of cold water shocked her momentarily, but she refused to adjust the temperature. She needed something to return her to reality.

For two days, she'd allowed herself to live in a fantasy world of romance and happily ever after, hoping that her knight in shining armor would declare his love for her and take her away to his castle, where they would fall deeper in love.

When the tears came, Carla was not surprised. She'd expected them. She knew that she needed to purge the rejection and sense of loss.

Minutes later, when she stepped out of the shower, she returned to being Carla Nevins, owner and director of a chain of travel agencies in Arlington, Virginia.

Widowed…and with no intention of marrying again.

No strings attached.

She needed to keep her resolve to remain single in focus. She'd allowed a silly holiday romance to tempt her from the straight road she'd mapped out for her life.

Losing her husband and child had devastated her and she'd vowed never to love anyone so much again. And here she was, after more than two years of living that vow, losing sight of the safe life she'd planned for herself.

Feeling like singing "I'm going to wash that man right out of my hair," she stepped back into the shower, but decided against the tune; singing was definitely not one of her talents.

Today, she would go on another of the scheduled tours around the island. Though she'd visited Barbados before, there were several places she wanted to see. Many of the guests spoke highly of the tours, so maybe that would be the perfect activity for the day. She could not resist the lure of the lush Barbadian countryside.

Since her travel agency specialized in Caribbean holidays, she frequented all the islands. However, a year didn't pass without her spending a few days in Barbados, soaking up the golden sunshine on one of its many beaches.

Her shower completed, Carla returned to the bedroom, quickly put on a pair of jeans, a T-shirt with the logo of her company on it and left the room, a wide smile on her face.

She had every intention of enjoying the rest of her stay in Barbados.

With or without Shayne Knight.

Shayne walked quickly along the corridor, his determination evident in his brisk stride. When his foreman had called him at the hotel, he'd been reluctant to leave, but he'd had no choice but to return to the plantation. One of the problems many of the plantation owners faced was the constant threat of fires. The increase this year in the seasonal hazard had been an annoyance, so when he'd received the call from Patrick last night, he'd intended to assess the damage quickly and return to the hotel.

However, when he'd arrived home, the fire had not only burned hundreds of acres, but had destroyed some homes on the perimeters of the cane fields. He'd spent the early hours of the morning extinguishing the blazes and dealing with the aftermath of the fires. Only, now, almost a day later, did memories of the past two days he'd spent with Carla come to mind.

Shayne promised himself that, as soon as he returned home, he'd call the hotel and convince the

One Gentle Knight

delectable Carla Nevins to stay on as his guest for an additional week. He wanted to get to know her better. In just a short space of time, the beautiful American had forced him to rethink his future and his determination to remain single. She had touched a long-forgotten part of him, and he knew he needed more than just a week of unbridled sex with her.

As Shayne reached the office of his lawyer, George Simpson, he knocked on the door, entering when the secretary buzzed him in.

"Morning, Mr. Knight, you can go right in. You're the first appointment for the morning."

"Thanks, Tina. How are you doing? Any word on when Jamar arrives from Trinidad?"

"I'm fine. I had planned to call you last week, but Mr. Simpson told me you were on holiday. Jamar's exams will be officially over on Friday this week and he arrives on Sunday. He can't wait to get back home and start work. Thanks for offering him the job."

"I have to thank him. He's a hard worker. When he worked for me during his holidays, I was very impressed by his great attitude. He has more than earned the position I offered him. You have a fine son."

"Thanks, Mr. Knight, I'm sure he'll be ready to start as soon as he comes home."

"I know he will be, but I'll let him start at the beginning of next month. I'm sure he needs a bit of recovery time before starting. Let him give me a call on Monday," he said, flashing her a rare smile. "I'll go into George now. Don't want to keep him waiting." He turned and headed toward George's office.

Before he could knock, a deep baritone responded. "Come in, Shayne. You're late."

As he entered the office, the phone rang. George, seated behind the desk that always seemed to swallow him, beckoned him to sit. Shayne never ceased to be amazed at the contrast between George's height and his James Earl Jones voice. Even the grandeur of the office seemed at odds with the short man lost within the large office chair.

However, despite his stature, which fooled many an opponent in court, George attacked each area of his life with the same confidence and enthusiasm. Instead of allowing his stature to affect him negatively, he used it to his advantage. As a result, his reputation as a trial lawyer allowed him to be selective when choosing clients.

When the phone conversation ended, he stood and extended his hand to Shayne, his grip firm. What George lacked in height, he made up for in mass. Five days a week in the gym had created a body of rippling muscles, which George used to seduce any woman with whom he came in contact.

"Glad to see you, Shayne." He smiled. "It's not often you pull yourself away from the plantation.

But, under the circumstances, it's understandable. When we've sorted out this problem, I'm going to want to hear about your week at the Hilton."

A naked Carla flashed before Shayne's eyes.

"The week was fine," Shayne responded. He tried to sound indifferent. "I did get some sleep and spent most of my time in bed, watching television," he offered.

Not the whole truth, but he really didn't want to answer any questions about Carla right now. George was one of his best friends and eventually he'd tell him, but he wasn't ready to talk about his mystery lover just yet.

"Sorry I had to come in so early this morning, but I wanted to deal with this situation as soon as possible. Have you found out the names of the families who lost their homes?"

"Yes, only two houses were destroyed. I hope you know that you're not legally responsible for what happened," George cautioned.

"I know, but did you get the information I asked for?" Shayne had expected George's assessment of the situation, but he had to make things right.

"Yes, I did and it's as you suspected. Neither of the families who lost their homes has insurance."

"I want you to make the necessary arrangements to have their homes rebuilt. Do they have anywhere to stay?"

"The Clarks will be staying with relatives, but the Greens have been staying at their neighbors and they're soon going to have to leave."

"I'll contact both families and make arrangements to assist them financially. Maybe having some money will help to take some of the strain they must be feeling. I'm sure it can't be easy for anyone to take them in."

"Are you sure you want to do this, Shayne?" George asked, his concern obvious. "It's going to be a lot of money."

"I understand your concern, George, but I have to do this. With the money my parents left and the money I've made in the past few years, giving them new homes and taking care of my tenants for a few months won't put a dent in what I have. This is something I have to do."

"Okay, but I'll make sure no one knows, as you requested. Can't let all those people know that, under that unsmiling exterior, there's really a gentle heart beating. Your secret is safe with me."

Shayne laughed. "Thanks, George. No wonder you're my lawyer. You know me better that anyone else. We've been best friends since our high-school days at The Lodge School; that's too long to reveal each other's secrets. Good thing you're not married. I'd have so many things to tell."

"Since I have no plans to get married anytime

soon, too many wild oats still to sow, it'll be a long time before you can disclose any secrets of mine."

"Anyway, as nice as it has been reminiscing about our boyhood and discussing your desire to remain unmarried, I have a lot to do today. I really don't want the Greens' lives disrupted too much. I want things to be as normal as possible for them, especially for the kids. I want them back at school in a day or two."

"Fine, I'll get things started on my end today. I'll give you a call later." George made a few notes on a legal pad.

"Good, thanks for working on this so quickly for me. I'm going to see what I can do about the increasing number of cane fires this year. Hopewell Plantation had a fire two days ago, and the circumstances are a bit suspicious. I spoke to Hopewell yesterday, and he's not too happy. I'm hoping this is not some crazy firebug trying to cause trouble."

A few minutes later, Shayne's silver SUV was speeding along the highway, heading toward the Knight Plantation in the parish of St. Thomas.

Despite his troubled thoughts, Shayne always enjoyed the drive home from the capital city of Barbados, Bridgetown. He loved his island, loved its history and loved the land. Unlike many of his friends who'd become doctors and lawyers, he'd always wanted to work on the plantation right alongside his father.

Now, driving along the rugged country road, miles and miles of cane fields stretched before him, he felt a sense of pride in what he'd accomplished. On an island where the sole dependence on sugar cane was no longer a reality, his success had made him a household name. In fact, as one of only two black men who owned plantations on the island, his success was often lauded in the local media. His success, however, would not have been possible if his father had not laid a strong foundation.

Dreams of his father and mother still came to him at night. However, they were no longer of the mangled car he'd been forced to see that night almost ten years ago. Now, the memories were of happy times of laughter and contentment.

The journey to this calm acceptance had been harder for Russell and Tamara, but he'd made sure they had the best counseling. They'd grown from awkward, angry adolescents, into confident, ambitious individuals. Neither had shown any interest in the land, but he made sure he'd helped them to go after their own dreams. He encouraged them to listen to and make their own music.

The land was his legacy—a legacy that only he could ensure would continue. He intended to pass on his love for the land to his son or daughter.

Children?

Carla Nevins had really worked her magic on

him. She'd made him think of wedding rings and happily ever after, of a mischievous little boy and a pretty little girl.

He'd done nothing to make sure that he had offspring. He'd spent most of his adult life taking care of Russell and Tamara. Yes, there had been women, but none that could be called a permanent fixture in his life. He had the occasional female friend. He took them out, spent a few hours in bed with them then returned home to his brother and sister. The women hadn't minded. None had wanted the responsibility of two teenagers. He soon realized there was no need to get married just to provide a mother figure for his sister and brother.

They had turned out quite well, under the circumstances. In fact, they were his pride and joy. Tamara was a bit of a tomboy, but she had become a beautiful young woman. She had decided to pursue a career in veterinary medicine in Jamaica.

Russell was already breaking hearts with his good looks. He, too, walked to the beat of his own drum. He'd decided to become a journalist. Russell was now working at a newspaper in New York while he did his postgraduate degree.

So, he needed to have children of his own. In fact, there was no guarantee that any kids of his would want to run a plantation, either, but he could hope. He did not want his family's legacy to end.

An image of a little boy perched on his back, as his father had carried him, flashed in his mind. He could also envision a woman and little girl standing on the verandah of plantation house, waving him goodbye as he went off to work each day.

He was not surprised that the woman was the spitting image of Carla Nevins, the woman who continued to haunt his every hour.

Immediately, he knew what he had to do. When this problem of the fires was all wrapped up, he'd return to the hotel. He was tired of being alone. During the few days with Carla, despite most of it being in bed, he'd caught a glimpse of the real woman. At moments of weakness, he experienced an overwhelming need to be gentle with her. He'd felt her cynicism, but he had also sensed profound sadness in her. What could have caused her so much grief?

He remembered kissing her tenderly on her cheeks, hoping she'd remain asleep. He had touched the smoothness of her hair and known that she was special. They'd not met under the most romantic of circumstances, but he knew he wanted that romance now. He wanted the courtship and the first date. And one other thing he knew: He needed her.

Perhaps, there was such a thing as happily ever after.

* * *

Shayne flipped his cell phone shut. There was still no response from the hotel room. He wondered where Carla had gone. The night before, he'd called his room at the hotel and, when there'd been no response, he'd called hers, only to have the voice mail answer each time.

He smiled.

She'd probably been sleeping so soundly, she didn't hear the phone. Like him, she must be tired after the exertions of the past few days.

No worry, in a few minutes he'd be back in her arms and ready to pick up where they'd left off. He was sure she'd be lying on the bed, naked and ready for him.

Already, he could imagine himself inside her.

He laughed.

What was wrong with him? He'd not been this horny since his late teen years. Now, in just a few days, he seemed no longer in control of his penis; it had a mind of its own.

When he pulled up in front of the Hilton several minutes later, he handed the valet the car keys, told him his room number and, in no time, stood in the elevator as it made its slow progress from floor to floor.

Before the elevator's doors could slide completely back, Shayne exited and hurried down the hallway. Reaching his room, he quickly slid the key card in and hurried inside when the door swung open.

The room was empty, the bed made. There was no evidence that she'd even been there.

Shayne glanced around the room, feeling a brooding sense of impending doom. He saw the flash of color—a sticky note on the mirror.

He crossed the room and picked it off in one fluid movement.

Shayne, I had a wonderful time, but it's time to get back to reality. Carla.

In that moment, rage as red and hot as fire burned inside him.

For some reason, he'd not expected this. She was gone. Maybe she hadn't felt anything special. He was a fool. He'd allowed himself to want more from what, to her, had been just a holiday romance.

There was nothing more.

No strings attached.

He was the one who wanted to change the rules, and, clearly, Carla saw things differently.

He wondered if she was still at the hotel. He'd go to her room. Deep down, he knew she'd felt something. He'd seen it in her eyes.

Instead, he picked up the phone and asked the receptionist to put him through to her room.

The words "Sir, Ms. Nevins checked out this morning," slapped him in the face, almost causing him to reel backward.

Checked out?

Why would she do that?

Time ticked by until Shayne realized he still held the phone in his hands.

A short while later, after a cold shower, he slipped between the covers, closed his eyes and willed himself to sleep.

Carla closed the magazine and turned her attention to the small screen before her. One more hour and she would be home. She was tired. The flight had been delayed for several hours at the Grantley Adams Airport and, when she'd finally boarded the plane, angry and frustrated, she'd been glad she'd chosen to fly first class.

She definitely needed the peace and quiet she knew she'd not get in economy class. From where she sat, she could hear the incessant crying of a baby.

She picked up the magazine for the umpteenth time, the silly antics of the actors on the small monitor not exactly what she wanted for the mood she was in.

She'd made the right decision. When Shayne had not returned that night, she'd tried to rationalize his behavior. The only thing she could think of was that he'd tired of her.

But she knew that wasn't true. She had seen glimpses of something more.

And she was not ready for it. The emotions she now experienced worried her, made her afraid. The days had become more that just a no-strings-attached liaison. They were the promise of something more. Something she was not ready for.

So she'd done the sensible thing. She'd packed her bags and ran.

Things had become too complicated.

She'd begun to feel something, something that she did not want to experience again.

The sex had been good enough, but the other emotion brought memories Carla didn't want, memories of her husband Richard and the loss she'd felt when he'd died. Carla remembered that night so clearly; it had been their anniversary and they were on their way to her favorite restaurant. The light had turned green, and Richard had pulled out.

Her next memory was of waking up to the sound of sirens and of blue flashing lights. Still trapped in the passenger's seat, she'd realized that her sense of disorientation was a result of the car being upside down. In the driver's seat, Richard's blank eyes had looked back at her, not seeing her.

The next time she'd awakened, it had been in the hospital.

Carla had not cried in the days leading up to the funerals of her husband and stillborn daughter and several weeks passed before, one night, in the stillness of yet another night of sleeplessness, she'd poured her heart out, finally allowing herself to grieve for her loss.

For two years, she had gone through the paces of her daily routine, the only comfort coming when she was with her friend, Sandra.

Carla knew that she used her job as a means of keeping the past buried. Being the owner and managing director of a chain of travel agencies across Virginia was a lot of work, and she made sure she didn't have time for much else, working often late into the night unless Sandra called to force her to leave and head home.

Carla had tried dating on a few occasions, preferring that to the constant nagging from Sandra and her other girlfriends, but none of her dates had been successful. She spent most of her time on a date comparing the men to Richard and finding them lacking.

In the past Carla might have found solace in her faith, but she believed God had failed her by allowing her husband and child to be taken. She no longer felt that overwhelming pounding anger, but her visits to the church she'd grown up in were rare oc-currences.

Now, in the past few days, she'd tried to wipe the memory of her husband from her mind. What scared her most was that it had worked. Shayne Knight had helped her to achieve what she'd been unable to do for two years: For a few hours, she'd not thought of Richard or the baby. Yes, the mem-ories had faded over the two years, but not a night passed that she didn't wake up to dreams of the crying of her child.

Carla turned her gaze outside.

Fluffy clouds beckoned her. The wide expanse of sky somehow provided comfort. Her short stay in Barbados hadn't ended as she'd wanted, but the time had changed her. She felt different. She felt changed, able to face her life as a stronger woman.

As soon as she reached home, she would take a long shower and call Sandra over. She felt like some time with her friend. She'd order a large pizza with all the garnishes they liked. Add a bottle of her favorite nonalcoholic wine, her favorite romantic comedy and the night would be perfect.

No men allowed.

Yes, that would clearly be her motto for the night.

When the plane touched down about noon, Carla

had already come to grips with her departure from Barbados, and she held her head high, ready to face the reality of her everyday world.

The memory of her days in Barbados would surely fade, in time.

Chapter 3

Three months later

Carla stared intently at the colored strip for the umpteenth time, unwilling to admit that what she'd suspected for a few weeks was true.

She was pregnant.

A couple of nights in paradise with a man she barely knew and her life had changed forever. In the weeks that followed her return to Virginia, Shayne had been constantly on her mind. His image, his scent and his touch still lingered, still stimulated each of her senses.

Now, a part of him was growing inside her. She

couldn't understand what had happened. She was sure they'd used protection…but, in reality, everything had become a blur after the first time. Ironically, she'd always been very adamant about the use of birth control.

With her first pregnancy, from the time she'd felt the stirring of her baby, she had fallen hopelessly in love with her unborn child. She never wanted to love like that again. The death of her little girl had devastated her.

What was she going to do?

She could have an abortion, but her strong beliefs ruled out that choice. Terminating her pregnancy was out of the question. She believed that individuals should take responsibility for the decisions they made in life, and she wouldn't be able to live with herself if she aborted a child.

Adoption was another alternative, but she already knew she wouldn't be able to give this child away. She'd examined the options because she wanted to be rational, but she wanted to keep her child. That much, she was sure about.

What she was unsure about was whether she should let Shayne know about her condition. She believed strongly in the importance of both parents in a child's life. She wasn't even sure what her plan was, but she could not deny her child a father. She'd go back to the island, find him and tell him about the baby.

But, no, that didn't make sense

She reached for her cell phone. Somehow she had to talk to someone. Her best friend, Sandra, should be at home right now. Sandra always gave her good advice.

Sandra picked the phone up on the first ring. "How's it going, girlfriend?"

"I'm pregnant."

"Girl, I didn't expect you to give me that answer right away. How about, 'I'm doing fine,' and then get down to the nitty-gritty?" Sandra paused, as if uncertain of what to say next. "How on earth did you get pregnant? I didn't even know you were having sex. I'm supposed to be your best friend and you had sex and didn't tell me?"

"Sandra, Sandra, will you please calm down."

"What do you mean, 'calm down'? So how'd it happen? You ain't had a man in months. Wait…did this happen in Barbados when you went there three months ago? Girlfriend, we have got to talk."

"Okay, okay, I'm sorry. I didn't tell you what happened. I just wanted to forget."

"I'm coming over now and you're going to tell me all the juicy stuff and more. You went to Barbados and had some loving and didn't tell me. Girl, I'm going to give it to you good when I get there.

I'm leaving now." All Carla heard was the click of disconnection.

Before Carla could put the kettle on to make a pot of coffee, she heard the screeching of car tires, quickly followed by the ringing of her doorbell.

When Carla opened the door, Sandra rushed in. Closing the door behind her, she immediately wrapped her arms around Carla. Tears were streaming down both of their faces.

An hour later, drained of most of the water in her body and after baring her soul, Carla was finally alone. Sandra had enjoyed listening to all the details of her liaison, and Carla had obliged her friend.

Her best friend had agreed with her decision to tell Shayne about the baby, but not before she'd called him a "dawg," and warned, "You better go on the Internet and see if you can find out anything 'bout him."

And that was exactly what Carla was about to do.

Switching her desktop computer on, Carla watched as the machine booted through its usual sequence. Logging onto the Internet, she narrowed her search for Shayne Knight by adding Barbados. Several links appeared and she clicked the first one.

An article from *National Geographic* on the sugar industry highlighted the significance of Shayne's revolutionary techniques to the success of his plantation and the slight surge in the profitability of the sugar industry.

However, an article from one of the local newspapers piqued her interest. Focusing on his status as one of Barbados' most eligible but elusive bachelors, the reporter also mentioned the tragic accident that had taken his parents' life. The article also stated that he'd undertaken running the family's plantation as well as caring for his younger brother and sister.

She could not help but be impressed by what she read, but she still had questions about her mystery man.

Would he acknowledge the baby? Would he make a good father? Would he accept her?

These were questions she could not answer now. She would leave for Barbados in a month or so. It would give her a chance to look at the situation before she made a definite decision. A month would also be enough time to make arrangements for someone to cover her work while she was gone.

Tired from reading so steadily on the computer, she glanced at her watch. Just after midnight. She needed to get some sleep. The day had been a stressful one and tomorrow would be no better. She'd made an appointment with a gynecologist Sandra had recommended. She didn't need any official confirmation, but she wanted to make sure that everything was all right. She didn't want anything to go wrong with this child.

During the day, the magnitude of having a life growing inside her had been an adrenaline rush. Tonight, in the quiet stillness of evening, the wonder of having a child growing in her was an awesome feeling.

She reached down to touch her stomach, her hand warm on her skin.

With a contented smile on her face, she drifted off to sleep.

But, in the world of dreams, *he* came to her.

Naked and virile.

A tall handsome man, skin kissed by the tropical sun.

Shayne flipped his cell phone shut and sighed. So, Carla owned a travel agency in Virginia—in Arlington, to be precise.

What was he going to do? Should he leave Barbados and go to Arlington? He had never been to Virginia. Maybe he could just make a call and apologize to her for disappearing so abruptly. Not that it made any sense at this point. Three whole months had passed since he'd made love to her and disappeared. He could only imagine how she'd felt when she'd woken up and found him gone. At the time, his only thought had been on the after effects of the fire and the families without homes.

A week after the fire, he had left for England to take part in talks with sugar buyers. That over, he'd flown over to France to spend some time with an old friend from school who now lived there.

Anything to put Carla Nevins from his mind.

With his busy schedule, the days were no problem. It was in the silent morning hours—when she came to him, her scent lingering in the air—that his memories of her were as vivid and clear as if she were next to him.

When he'd returned home a week ago, he'd known he had to do something about his state of mind before he went crazy.

He had to find her.

Now, he had as much information as he could get on her. The private investigator he'd hired had done a good job. He'd been pleased with the report the man had placed in his hand just this morning.

Shayne pulled onto the highway, joining the heavy traffic until he took the road north to St. Thomas.

A mile before his home, he turned into a small village nestled in the dense cane fields. Following the directions he'd received from George, he easily found the house where the Greens were staying.

Outside, two children sat playing. He parked the

car and moved cautiously toward the house, pausing briefly to say hi to the kids. The boy responded with a shy smile, while the little girl stared at him with wide, wary eyes.

"I'm looking for Joanne Green."

"That's our mommy," the boy replied. "She's inside with our aunt. She sent us outside to play."

"Can you go call her for me? Tell her that Mr. Knight is here to see her."

"Okay," the boy said, before he turned and raced into the house.

He glanced down at the girl, her head now bent, playing with a doll that bore a striking resemblance to Tyra Banks. She looked up, her eyes still wary.

"I saved my doll from the fire. My mom says I'm a brave girl, but I miss Snuggles. He got burned."

Not sure who Snuggles was, Shayne responded the only way he could. "I think you're a brave girl, too. I'm sure Snuggles is happy in heaven."

"You promise?" Hope replaced the wariness he'd seen in her eyes.

"I promise."

At the same time, the boy returned with a slightly plump woman.

"I'm Joanne Green," she said when she reached him, stretching out a hand to shake his. "I'm glad to finally meet you. What you're doing for us is more than I expected. I don't know how I could ever repay you." With that she started to cry, but quickly composed herself. "I don't worry too much about myself, but I wasn't too sure I could stay here with my neighbor much longer. I didn't want to overstay my welcome. I know she doesn't mind, but the house is barely big enough for her and her kids."

"I'm glad that I could help," Shayne said. "Tonight, I'll send someone over to collect you and take you to the cottage I've had fixed up for you. I'll come and see you sometime tomorrow, after you've settled in. I bought some things for the kids while I was in England. I hope they'll like them."

"Mr. Knight, I'm sure they will be pleased with your gifts. I don't know how to thank you."

"Think nothing of it. It's the least I can do." Beginning to feel a bit embarrassed, he decided that it was time he left. "I have to be off. There are quite a few things I have to do to ensure all is ready when you arrive. I'll see you in the morning."

As he turned to walk away the little girl rushed to him and placed her hand in his, her face serious with purpose. "Thank you, Mr. Knight. I'll talk to Snuggles tonight when I say my prayers, since he's in heaven."

"That's good. I'm sure he'll hear you. Promise you'll come look for me at the plantation house," he said. "As long as your mother approves."

"You've already done enough, Mr. Knight. I don't want them bothering you."

"They'll be no bother. I have a younger brother and sister and much of their childhood stuff is still there. And, of course, I can take them to the video shop."

Glancing down at his watch, he realized that he needed to get back to the plantation.

"Well, I really have to go. Bye, Mrs. Green. Bye, kids."

As Shayne drove away, he glanced at the three waving at him in the rearview mirror. He didn't know what had come over him. He rarely had much to do with kids, didn't particularly care for them, but there was something about the young Greens that struck a chord. They reminded him of Russell and Tamara. They were way younger than his brother and sister had been when his parents had died, but their vulnerability struck a cord with him.

At the funeral, holding Tamara had not been a surprise. His sister was the emotional one, and she'd easily given in to tears.

Russell had tried to be so strong. Too strong.

That same night, after the wake, when all the family had departed, Shayne went to his favorite spot on the plantation—a pond hidden in the midst of a patch of banana trees. He'd sat there into the early hours of the morning.

Later, after returning to the house, he'd been passing his brother's room when he'd heard the slightest of whimpers. He'd pushed the door only to find his brother curled in a tight ball, trying to hide his grief under a pillow. That night, his relationship with his brother had changed. Though they'd always been friends, that night, his so-brave-I'm-a-man-now-brother had wrapped his arms around him and bawled his eyes out.

Fortunately, Tamara had been spending the night with her best friend, so they'd both had a good cry. Shayne had held his brother until he'd finally fallen asleep.

The next morning they'd talked, really talked and he'd learned so much about his brother. Russell had told Shayne all about his dreams and aspirations.

His heart soared with pride. His brother had turned out well. Head boy of his secondary school and an island scholar at sixteen, Russell was every parent's dream, but Shayne still worried about him. Russell never seemed to have time for anything but his books. Studying was his life. Even though Shayne would have preferred that the boy be more social, he decided to leave him alone. He knew that his brother would eventually sort his life out.

Tamara, too, loved to study and had been an island scholar the year immediately after Russell.

But in personality they were totally different. While Russell was an introvert and kept to himself, Tamara loved life and lived it to the fullest. She was involved in sports, sang in the church choir and still had time to do her schoolwork.

They were both good kids, but they no longer needed him. Now it was time he made a life for himself. And maybe his new life included the elusive Carla Nevins.

Maybe, he could take a chance with Carla.

Carla closed the door and walked into the warm sunshine. Arlington during the summer reminded her a bit of the islands. Outside, she headed to the small restaurant just across the road from the doctor's office. She now had confirmation that she was pregnant—not that she'd had any doubt.

Three months pregnant almost to the day.

Carla laughed at the irony of the situation. They'd both wanted a no-strings-attached affair, but destiny had played them and now here she was single and pregnant.

A part of her felt ashamed of what she'd done. Despite her recent poor attendance at church, she had grown up with strong spiritual principles.

But she had no one to blame but herself. She'd allowed herself to be consumed by the death of her husband and child. Without even realizing it, she'd

existed in a state of limbo, somewhere between depressed and feeling okay, but never feeling good
enough to do anything stupid.

Well, this was still an indication that she'd not
been thinking well. Carla realized the folly of her
impulsive trip to Barbados. She'd acted so completely out of character, and she'd not come out of
it unscathed. The baby growing inside her was clear
evidence of what she'd done.

She wondered if the child would take after her
or if he or she would be blessed with a combination of the best features of her family and Shayne's.

On reflection, it really didn't matter what he or
she looked like. Her only prayer was for a healthy
child.

A month later, Carla snapped her seat belt in
place and prepared for her flight to Barbados. To
say that she felt apprehensive was an understate-
ment. She was terrified, but she knew that her decision to confront Shayne with her pregnancy was
the right thing to do. After a lengthy discussion
with Sandra, and an even lengthier one with herself, she had finally taken the steps to go back to
the island.

In the past four weeks, Carla had worked tire-
lessly to make sure that, when she left the agency,
Sandra would not have to deal with any problems.

They hired a temporary assistant to help Sandra with the administrative work involved in running the business.

Carla had also tried to prepare herself for the emotional roller coaster, which she now rode. Accepting the pregnancy had been easier than she thought.

Looking back, she realized the risk she'd taken when she had gone to bed with a stranger. Her behavior had been so out of character. There was no justification for what she had done, but now that was water under the bridge.

She'd made the choice to go to Barbados and tell Shayne about her…their child and now she had to go through with her decision.

She could not deny him his child, nor could she deny her child a father. She wanted the baby she carried to know the love of a father.

Her only reservation was her uncertainty about Shayne's reaction. Would he toss her out? Would he deny the child was his?

These questions had haunted her until she'd made the decision to go. And they continued to haunt her as she boarded the plane.

Now, she was haunted by the memory of a man who'd made love to her with the fervor and passion of a man born to be her lover.

In the still of the night, when sleep had failed to

come, she'd been haunted by the image of a man with eyes as black as night and flaming with desire.

Four hours later, the flight touched down at Grantley Adams Airport, and Carla sighed deeply. She was here. Tonight she'd spend the time at a hotel on the south coast where she'd made reservations. Tomorrow, she'd call a taxi to take her to the Knight Plantation and, she hoped, her journey here would start to make sense.

Tonight, her head hurt from the tension and stress of the past few weeks. But Carla knew she'd done the right thing.

She only hoped that Shayne Knight felt the same way.

Two days later, Shayne left an important meeting with several of the plantation owners and sugar producers on the island. He felt that they were finally coming to an agreement on the issue that had been hovering in the background for the past few months.

The talks in England with sugar buyers had proven to be successful and he felt positive about the direction of the fading sugar industry on the island. A meeting with the Ministry of Agriculture and several island officials had been equally successful. He and the other plantation owners realized that the government was finally listening to them.

Feeling a bit on top of the world, Shayne turned his silver SUV into his driveway and was surprised to see a taxi heading in the opposite direction.

A visitor?

He wasn't expecting anyone. He rarely had visitors and the few family members who lived on the island had their own cars and rarely visited unannounced.

Shayne quickly parked at the rear of the house and used the kitchen entrance to his home. Gladys greeted him with her usual smile, though she seemed concerned about something.

Before he could ask her about the taxi, she said, "Shayne, you have a visitor. She just arrived. Said she's a friend. I put her in the sitting room and gave her a glass of lemonade. She doesn't seem well. I think the heat's a bit too much for her, so I turned the air conditioning on."

This was getting stranger by the minute. Maybe it was someone from… Hell, he didn't know. The best way to find out would be to go to the sitting room.

Assuring Gladys that all would be well, he exited the kitchen and quickly made his way along the hallway.

Outside the room, Shayne paused briefly, noticing the woman standing before a painting of his mother and father over the large sofa where he often fell asleep. There was something vaguely familiar about her. It may have been the way she stood, the way she held her head....

As if sensing his presence, she turned slowly and his heart stopped.

Carla stood before him, her expression uncertain.

"From the look on your face, I'm sure that I'm the last person you expected to see, Shayne," she said. Her sarcasm did not fail to reach him.

For a moment, she stood silently.

Then, like a scene in one of those daytime soap operas Tamara was addicted to, Carla, the woman who'd haunted his dreams, crumpled floorward.

Shayne sprinted across the room, catching Carla just before she fell to the ground.

Holding her in his arms, he walked briskly, amazed at how fragile she was. Shayne could tell she'd lost weight. Her arms were narrower and her face appeared gaunt. His gaze moved downward, noticing her full rounded breasts and her...

Shayne almost dropped her.

Carla was pregnant!

Her condition had not been apparent at first, but holding her in his arms made him aware of the gentle mound that now replaced the flat, firm stomach he remembered.

She was pregnant!

What the hell was going on?

Why was she here?

Each question drummed in his head, keeping time with the steady beat of his footsteps as he mounted the stairs and headed straight to the master bedroom.

Placing her on his bed, Shayne dialed the intercom and barked orders into it. When a startled Gladys responded to his call, Shayne directed her to call the doctor immediately.

Damn, he'd have to apologize to Gladys when he had Carla settled, but he preferred not to leave her in this room. This was his sanctuary and knowing his past with her, he didn't want her disturbing the peace he'd finally restored to his well-ordered life.

He glanced at her as she lay unconscious, her chest heaving with her ragged breathing. He hoped Troy would soon be here. One of the advantages of having a best friend who was a doctor was having him at your beck and call. Not that he did it often, but Tamara had been prone to injuries with her daring approach to sports and life.

Carla groaned and then she reached out, grabbing a pillow and pulling it close to her.

She was pregnant!

The child was his.

He had no doubt that was the reason she was here.

Damn, what had he done? He wasn't ready for this. *How had it happened?*

A silly question, but he was sure they'd used protection. But they'd made love so many times, he'd lost count.

The ringing of his cell phone forced him from his troubled thoughts.

"Hello," he said, trying to control his need to shout.

"Shayne, I'm on my way. I just passed the gas station in Redman Village. What's the problem? Gladys left a message about some woman fainting."

"Yeah, my baby's mother just fainted in my arms."

"Baby's mother? Shayne, what the hell are you talking about? You got some woman pregnant? How? You been drinking, boy? You know you can't hold no liquor."

"No, I mean, yes… Listen, Troy, let's not talk about this right now. I'll tell you everything when you get here."

"Yeah, you definitely have a lot of explaining to do. I'll be there in five."

Troy disconnected and Shayne placed the phone on the mahogany desk.

He lowered himself onto the chair and placed his head on the desk.

This was a bit more than he could handle just now. What had happened to his perfect day and what the hell was he going to do about Carla?

An hour later, Shayne watched as his best friend's car drove down the driveway and pulled onto the main road. Troy had taken care of Carla, informing him that she needed to eat properly and that she needed to take things easy for a week or so.

And, yes, that she was definitely pregnant.

Carla had awoken for a few minutes, looked around the room, smiled and then had gone back to sleep.

He'd spent the next half hour telling Troy about his "vacation" a few months ago.

Of course, Troy had wanted graphic details, but Shayne'd refused to say much about his time with Carla, providing only the bare facts. Troy had finally left with a silly smile on his face.

"Bye, Papa," he'd shouted as he drove away.

Shayne pulled a magazine from the nearby bookcase and slipped into the ancient rocking chair his mother had sat in when telling him nightly bedtime stories.

He'd sit here and wait patiently until Carla woke up. There was a lot he had to find out.

Most of all, he wanted to hear from Carla that the child was his.

* * *

Gladys sat in her room, her gaze focused on a picture of Shayne, Russell and Tamara, which held a place of honor on her mantel.

What was going on? Who was the woman who had fainted? And what was she to Shayne?

When the woman had arrived this afternoon, Gladys had been a bit surprised. The slight mound about her waist had sent off warning bells in Gladys's head.

At first, Gladys wondered if she was some conniving gold-digger trying to work a smart con on Shayne, but then she'd realized the woman was nervous and very frail. Gladys could tell she needed a good meal.

And then Gladys had taken a probing look into her eyes and had seen a woman who was scared, and she'd felt her caution melt.

She wasn't sure what Shayne had done, but she knew that this woman was just what Shayne needed.

Yeah, she could tell there was stuff that needed to be discussed, but, as she always said, "God will take care of everything."

She was going to enjoy watching how this situation worked itself out. It might take a while, but she intended to start looking for a dress. Preferably a pink one. There was nothing more stunning than a pink dress at a wedding.

Chapter 4

Carla slowly opened her eyes. The pain in her head was unbearable. At first, everything appeared fuzzy but, when her vision cleared, she was able to make out the man sitting next to the bed.

For a moment, she tried to remember why she was lying in a strange bed with Shayne Knight sitting in a chair watching her. And then she remembered the melodramatic soap-opera moment when she had crumpled to the floor. She couldn't believe what had happened to her.

"It's not often that a woman ends up in my bed on her first visit to my home," he said, a hint of laughter in his voice.

Carla didn't smile.

Images of the two of them wrapped in each other's arms just a few short months ago reminded her that what he said was not strictly true. Yeah, technically, the bed hadn't been his, but arguing about the semantics of what he said would only make her more embarrassed about the situation.

She'd made a mistake. She'd been silly to come here. Returning to the island in hopes that Shayne would do the right thing was a bit too much, even for her.

Their coming together had brought intense pleasure, but they'd both made sure that the pleasure came with no strings attached. Little did she anticipate that she'd be pregnant and back in Barbados in a few short months.

When she finally spoke, her words were strained.

"I'm sorry. I shouldn't have come. It was silly of me. You have your life, your family. I remember what you said when we met at the hotel. You didn't want any complications in your life. No wife or kids. And here I come, forcing a child on you."

"Forcing!" She heard a hint of anger in his voice. "I'd prefer you not to talk about our child like that. I'd never consider a child of mine to be forced on me."

Again, Carla didn't know what to say. She'd not expected this reaction, but some of the fear she'd felt just slid a notch.

"How're you feeling?" he asked.

"Hungry."

Shayne smiled.

"I'll get Gladys to bring you something to eat," he said. "There are leftovers from lunch."

"A large glass of lemonade would be nice."

Carla watched as Shayne walked over to a small desk, lifted the phone and spoke to someone on the other line.

"Your lemonade will soon be here, but I've asked Gladys to send a light snack. You need to eat," he said. "For the baby."

She didn't argue. He was right. She'd not eaten since she'd left the airport in Virginia that morning. Her flight to Miami and then on to Barbados had taken most of the day, but she'd felt no urge to eat the generic fare offered on either of the flights. Instead, she'd settled for a small cup of latte in Miami, but now the hollow sensation in her stomach told her that she was really hungry.

She had to remember she was now eating for two and the tiny life inside was already showing evidence of a voracious appetite.

There was a knock on the door and Shayne moved to it. He opened the door and took a tray from a woman who stood just outside the room.

He returned to the chair, this time turning it around and straddling it.

"Can you feed yourself? I'm willing to help."

"No, I can handle it. Just stay and keep me company."

Before the words slipped from her lips, Carla heard her request in her head and was mortified.

Her gaze moved to his face and she was not surprised when she saw the hint of amusement in his eyes.

"You can go if you have to. I don't want to be the one responsible for taking you from your work. I'll be fine," she said.

At first, it seemed he would stay, but then he rose from the chair and stretched.

"I do have a few things I have to do before nightfall. I'll let you eat in peace, but we will talk tonight. They are a lot of things we have to talk about, but I'll let you take your rest now. Would you like to stay in the room for dinner later or do you want to eat in the dining room with me? If you want to join me, please call someone to help you down to the dining room. I'll send Gladys up for you."

With that, he turned and headed for the door, only glancing back at her one final time, before leaving the room.

Shayne closed the door behind him. For some reason, he wanted to get out of the room as quickly as he could. He had work in his office he needed to take care of, but his need to get away from Carla was greater. He'd realized something in the time he'd sat looking at her. His feelings for her went deeper that he expected or wanted. It wasn't only about what had happened between them. It wasn't even about the baby. He wasn't sure *what* it was about. All he knew, was that there was a part of him that wanted Carla in his life.

Thinking about her over the past few months was totally different from seeing her lying on his bed.

She might appear fragile now, but Carla was one of the strongest and the most beautiful women he knew. Shayne loved the combination of her soft caramel skin and the dark mahogany of her hair, which fell just below her shoulders.

Her eyes sparked with life and passion, while the gentle yet firm curve of her cheekbones hinted at her confidence and her stubbornness. As she lay on his bed, however, no evidence of Carla's true nature showed. Instead, she was a woman who appeared vulnerable and troubled by what she must be dealing with, and he felt a deep shame at his part in her situation.

Like him, she'd made it clear that children were no part of her plan for life. She seemed to be happy with life as a single woman and she seemed devoted to her business. She appeared to have no time for distractions.

And their coming together had been a distraction neither of them could afford. The consequences of his passion were now readily apparent, and he wondered how it would all end.

He wondered what Carla must be feeling and what she wanted from him.

At least, she'd come to him. He was glad for that. If this were a romance novel, this story would probably start years down the road with his discovering that he was the father of a teenage boy or girl. Fortunately, this was real life and he would forever be grateful to Carla for coming back to Barbados.

But he was scared. He knew nothing about being a father. Yes, he'd taken care of Russell and Tamara, but, at the time of their parents' death, they had already been in their teens. This was different, and he wasn't sure what would be expected of him. He didn't have anyone he could talk to about the situation.

He wasn't even sure if he wanted a baby in his life. Despite denying that she'd be forcing a child on him, the thought of a child in his life was frightening. Yes, he'd let her stay around until their baby was born, but as soon as she could return home he'd set her up with a comfortable allowance and return to his hectic but uncomplicated bachelor life.

Shayne went directly to the kitchen, his stomach finally making him aware he'd not eaten since lunch. His focus had been on Carla and making sure she was all right.

Gladys met him at the entrance to the kitchen, the table was heavily laden with his favorite foods.

"Gladys," he said, "I want you to make sure Carla eats something, too. She needs to eat." He looked at the woman fondly. He loved Gladys as if she were his second mother. He could not have handled his parents' death and raising his brother and sister without Gladys. He needed to tell her what was going on, but he would do it later.

He could see the look in her eyes. She wanted to know what was going on.

"We'll talk later," he promised. "Go up and stay with her for a while."

Gladys nodded, her eyes locking with his, and then she walked away, but not before he saw the look of concern on her face.

He piled a plate with the Gladys' special spicy chicken wings and vegetable stir-fried rice. He ate slowly, trying to focus on the meal and clearing his mind of the events of the evening. He needed to get to his office to complete the report requested by the Ministry of Agriculture, and then he'd get some much-deserved rest.

When he was done, he cleaned up the kitchen and headed for his home office.

He entered the room and opened the window,

letting the cool night air in. For a moment, he stood at the window.

The night was a gentle one, with the full moon casting its rays on the vast mahogany trees, which surrounded the main house.

In the distance, he could see the lights of his foreman's house. Inside, he knew Patrick would be spending time with his wife and kids. Patrick should be proud of his family. He had a beautiful wife, Monica, whom he adored, and two sons— Connor and Christopher, who were his pride and joy. Shayne always felt a twinge of envy whenever he was around Patrick's family.

Since he had no intention of getting married, he buried the unwanted emotion deep within him, preferring to accept that some people were made for love, and he was definitely not one of them.

The lights in Patrick's house flicked off and Shayne moved away from the window, turning to glance at the clock. It was almost ten o'clock. He needed to get some work done.

Before he could sit, Gladys entered the room. She carried a tray bearing his nightly cup of tea.

Placing the tray on a nearby desk, she handed the cup to him.

As Shayne took it, he noticed her broad smile, but he was not fooled by it. Gladys was here on a fact-finding mission.

"Is it your child?" she asked, taking a seat on the couch. From her expression, Shayne could tell that the question was rhetorical, but he answered her, anyway.

"Yes," Shayne replied. There was no sense in denying it. "I met her that weekend I stayed at the Hilton."

"You're going to be a father," she said. "Didn't I teach you the importance of using protection?" She wagged a finger at him sternly.

"Yes, you did. I was sure I used protection, but some of the weekend is a bit blurred." He blushed, embarrassed by the nature of the conversation, but Gladys didn't seem to notice. Her eyes were dull with disappointment. "I'm sorry. I don't know what happened that weekend. I didn't plan for it to happen. I'm sure Carla didn't, either.

"I'm not sure what her motive for coming is, but I'm glad she came. I wouldn't want any child of mine to grow up not knowing his father."

"So you're going to do the right thing?" Gladys asked.

"The right thing?" Shayne heard an alarm going off in his head.

"Yes, the right thing! Marry her." Her voice was calm and firm.

Somehow, he hadn't thought that far ahead, but, as far as he was concerned, marriage was not part of the picture. Marriage presented too many problems and complications and his parents' own rocky marriage had only served to emphasize the fickle nature of love and marriage. He'd leave that noble institution to men like Patrick.

"How do you know she wants marriage? Maybe she just wants support. Maybe she wants money."

In the instant he said it, Shayne knew that was not the case with Carla. Though their acquaintance was brief, it had been intense, and he guessed he knew her pretty well. And he would bet his life on it—Carla was not a gold-digger. "I shouldn't have said that. I'm sure she's not after my money. I get the impression her business is doing quite well."

"So you're not sure what you're going to do?"

"Gladys, right now, I don't have a clue, but, when I do, I promise you I'll make a mature responsible decision."

"That's all I can ask of you. She does seem like a nice girl."

"She is. I have no doubt about that."

"Then, there's nothing else for me to say here. You have a good night." Gladys bent over and kissed him and then she left, humming one of her favorite gospel tunes.

Shayne was left alone with thoughts of what had transpired during the day.

* * *

The next time Carla woke up, it was to the sound of a bird pecking outside the window. The now familiar wave of nausea greeted her when she tried to stand, causing her to inhale deeply. She hoped that this sickness that came with her pregnancy wouldn't last much longer. She felt awful and she couldn't call what she had morning sickness because her bouts of queasiness were not limited to the mornings. They came at any time of the day.

However, her current state did little to diminish her feeling about the child growing inside her. Already, she was in love with the baby, basking in the knowledge that she was being given a second chance to be a mother. She was also scared. The thought of motherhood was daunting, but she knew she'd be a good mother.

If only nothing went wrong….

The fact that she'd lost a baby before made her cautious. She wanted so desperately for everything to go well. She had every intention of making sure she followed the doctor's orders to the letter.

But her feelings of well-being were also threatened by new fears. What if Shayne decided he wanted full custody of the child? What if he had lied about not being married and had a wife and lots of children?

All those questions had delayed her decision to come to Barbados, but she'd finally decided that coming here was the right thing to do. She had no idea where her life was heading. Somehow, this situation had interrupted her plans for the future. A child was definitely not a part of the wider picture.

Neither was the brooding, silent Shayne Knight.

Whoever said all knights came in shining armor?

Shayne picked up the phone and dialed the still-unfamiliar number. On the first ring, Russell's voice came over the line.

"Yo," came the familiar greeting. Shayne felt his heart tighten. "What's goin' on, big bro?"

He wished his brother would discontinue all the youthful slang, but he knew it wouldn't happen anytime soon. And he knew that he was demonstrating the same biased attitudes that he hated. He couldn't help it. Remnants of his colonial education still lingered.

His brother and sister were from a generation of kids who embraced the African-American way of life and culture. They'd assimilated its lingo, its music and its very essence. It was a struggle, but he'd tried with all of his power to make sure his siblings learned as much as possible about their own culture and history.

"Yo, back at you," he responded. As expected, Russell laughed at his attempt at being cool. It was a longstanding joke between the two of them.

"So what's going on?" his brother asked.

"I'm fine, but I think you better sit for this one. I have some news for you."

"Okay, I'm sitting. Shoot."

He hesitated. This wasn't as easy as he'd thought it might be. He really wasn't sure how to share the news.

"Shayne, what's the matter?" Russell's voice held concern.

"I'm going to have a baby," he finally responded, and winced when he heard the loud bark of laughter.

"Russell, don't be silly. You know what I mean."

"How the hell did that happen? Tamara and I leave you alone for a hot second and you go and get yourself in trouble. Man, you must have been thirsty."

"I won't have your disrespect, boy."

"Sorry, Shayne, I didn't mean to laugh, but I would still like to know how this miracle occurred." Shayne heard a muffled snort. It was obvious Russell was trying not to laugh again.

"Remember, after you left, I spent some days at the Hilton during its opening week? I met a woman there, we spent most of the weekend in bed and now, she's back on the island. Pregnant."

"You sure it's yours?" Russell asked.

"Yes," Shayne said in exasperation. "Carla is not like that. I know the baby's mine."

"So what are you going to do? You've never wanted children. You've never even talked about getting married."

"I'm not sure what I'm going to do right now. I've invited Carla to stay here until the baby's born. After she has it, she can go back to the States. Of course, I'll get George to make the necessary financial arrangements."

"So you're determined not to get married? I think you would make a good husband and father."

"Russell, I may have taken care of you and Tamara, but I don't know anything about being a father. I'm not even sure if I want to be one. I don't have the time to be a father. I barely have time to do all the work around here."

"Seems you've made up your mind about what you want to do. I'm sure any advice that I have to offer would be of no consequence."

Shayne heard the censure in his brother's voice.

"No, I want to hear what you think."

"I'm not thinking much, but one thing I know, I wouldn't want some other man raising my child."

"I wasn't your father. I raised the two of you and you both turned out fine."

"Yeah, we did, but that was different."

"True, I didn't have a choice."

Russell's silence made him aware of what he'd said.

"Russ, I didn't mean it in that way. I did have a choice, and I chose to take care of you and Tamara. Both of you know I'd do anything for you."

It was only when he stopped, thinking of how to appease his brother that he realized Russell was attempting to stifle his laughter.

"Shayne, you're so square. Tamara and I know how much you love us. I'm sure we'd never be able to repay you for what you did, but, I, for one, don't want to see you lonely and alone in your old age. And I still think you'd make a wonderful father. I have firsthand experience of your parenting skills.

Shayne smiled, his moment of trepidation past.

"So tell me a bit about this Carla. Is she pretty? Sexy? Nice firm breasts? I know you like them that way."

About to protest his brother's nosiness, Shayne decided, instead, to answer the questions.

"Yes, she's fine. Definitely. All the above."

"So what are you waiting on, bro? Go for it. I predict you'll be married before the year is over."

"I can promise you that won't ever happen. You have my word on it."

"So you say. Hey, big bro, I have to go. Big test tomorrow. You spoken to Tamara recently?"

"No, but she did e-mail to tell me she was doing fine and recently aced one of her midterms."

"Good, she said a few days ago she hadn't heard from you in a while. Want me to tell her about the baby?"

"No, thanks. I'll tell her myself. I don't want her to come rushing back home. You know she believes that she has to make sure we both stay responsible."

"Yeah, I know. That's why I made sure I didn't go to the same university she did. She'd be making sure I took my vitamins and that my underwear was clean."

Shayne laughed. "I know what you mean."

For a moment, they were both silent.

"I miss her, Shayne. And you, I miss you, too."

"I wish I could say the same thing little, bro. But I'm happy to have the two of you out of the house. I'm embracing my freedom."

"Yeah, sure," Russell replied.

"Of course, I miss the two of you. I love you both."

"Love you, too, Shayne, but let's get back to the matter at hand. What are you going to do about this baby?"

"I'm not sure. I'll make sure Carla has everything she needs for the child, but I'm not ready to give up my freedom. Maybe I'll get more involved in his life when he gets older. He can come visit me a week or two each summer. When you and Tamara are home, you can help take care of him."

"Oh, so we're to take care of your child while you're at work?"

"Maybe Carla can come with him when he comes each summer. I'll make sure I do some of the fatherly stuff and have 'quality time' with him each visit."

"Shayne, I think you'd better stop before I get really annoyed. You're going to have to take care of your own little one. Of course, I'll be the perfect uncle, but I definitely don't want to be a substitute dad. I can't imagine how you raised Tamara and me with this whack attitude toward parenting."

"Maybe I did a better job than I thought," Shayne replied, with just a hint of laughter. "Well, Russell, you did say you had to go and I have a few important business calls I have to make."

"Okay, you go do your work. Enjoy what's left of the day. Love you, bro."

Before Shayne could respond, he heard the quick click of disconnection and knew his brother was gone.

Alone again, Shayne began to expand on his parenthood plan. He could learn to be a father. He would go to the library and borrow some books about pregnancy and parenting. Maybe by the time the baby was born, he would know a bit of what he needed. It would be simple. He'd learn to be a father and, since he wouldn't be one for more than a few weeks each year, the arrangement would be perfect.

He exited his office and headed straight for the room he'd placed Carla in. When he knocked on the door, there was no response. He knocked again, this time pushing the door gently open before he entered.

Carla lay asleep on the bed, her hair spread on the pillow beneath her head.

His arousal came hard and fast. He groaned with frustration. What was he going to do? She still had the same intense effect on him, making him lose his cool at the very sight of her. Right now, she was simply sleeping as innocently as the baby she carried in her womb, and just watching her sent his body into overdrive.

The image of a child suckling on her breast came to mind. This was definitely not what he wanted. He didn't want or need this. Already, this baby was changing his life.

He wondered if the child would look like him or her. Not that it mattered one way or the other. He just wanted her to have a healthy child.

Damn, he didn't seem to have a clue what he wanted. One minute, he was willing to place his child's upbringing in another person's hand and, in the next breath, he was wondering who the child would look like.

Strolling over to the chair next to the bed, Shayne sat quietly, not wanting to wake Carla. She needed to sleep.

He reached over for the blanket at the bottom of the bed, unfolded it and placed it over her. The air-conditioning was on and the room felt cool and comfortable. He'd stay and make sure she was all right before he left for the night. He might have doubts about his parenting skills, but the baby was still his. He would do his best to ensure that Carla and his child had the best of care.

When Shayne opened his eyes, the scent of a woman wafted into his nostrils. For a moment, he was disoriented. Then he remembered he'd lain down on the bed with her when Carla had started to toss and turn. During the night, she'd curled herself around him and he could feel the definite outline of her breasts against his body.

Again, a flash of desire pierced down to his groin. What was he going to do?

Even though he'd responded to Russell's questions with the assertion that he would do what was best, he didn't feel sure about his convictions. Carla had turned his comfortable existence upside-down. Shayne knew, beyond a shadow of doubt, that his life was changing.

Now, feeling restless and uneasy, Shayne rose

from the bed and crept from the room. He moved toward his office, willing himself to think about the details of running the plantation.

On the way there, he changed directions. He wouldn't be able to concentrate until he did something to relieve the tension in his body.

Shayne exited the house from the rear, following the gravel path that lead to the stables. There he found his horse, Mongoose, and several mounts he'd purchased for use by the occasional business visitor who wanted to tour the dense natural woodland around the plantation.

Mongoose whinnied when Shayne appeared. A solid-black Arabian, she stood at almost fifteen hands. She was never happier than when she was racing across the wide expanse of land that surrounded the plantation.

"Miss me, girl? I know I've not been around recently, but I've been really busy." At the horse's look of reprimand, he felt a sense of loss. "I know I'm making excuses, but I promise it won't happen again. Want to go for a ride?"

He watched for the telltale spark of excitement in the horse's eyes before he reached for a saddle and rested it gently on the horse's back.

A few minutes later, he and the horse were flying in the wind, the horse's hooves barely touching the ground.

* * *

Carla slipped from the bed as soon as she heard Shayne's footsteps in the hallway. His attempt to leave quietly had been unsuccessful since the click of the lock when he closed the door had echoed in the room.

She walked toward the window and opened it. The morning breeze caressed her, startling her with its nippiness. As her body adjusted to its slight chill, she felt herself coming alive. Carla stretched. She felt much better than she had the day before.

Her eyes browsed the landscape, taking in the buildings that made up the plantation. She knew that plantations on the island were large. Changes in the island's economy, from sugar to tourism, made it possible for only a handful of big sugar operations to survive. She already knew that the Knight Plantation was one of the most productive on the island.

A flash of color to the right of the main house caught her attention and she watched as Shayne appeared from the stables leading a large black horse. Mesmerized, Carla watched as he mounted the horse with the grace of a skilled jockey. Horse and rider trotted slowly out of the compound. She watched them as they moved farther away and then the horse broke into a gallop. They eventually disappeared behind the dense shrubbery in the distance.

She'd just discovered another facet of the man whose child she carried. Here she was, several months pregnant from a man who was still a mystery to her. She wondered what kind of man he was. She wanted to know the father of her child. She *needed* to know more about him. What made him tick? What made him ride a horse like the wind across a windswept tropical landscape?

The more she thought about him, the more she wondered if he would make a good father. She knew he had no intentions of allowing the child into his life. He'd made it quite clear that he'd tolerate her and the child, but only until her baby was old enough to fly back to the United States.

Maybe he'd come around after their child was born.

Damn, was she crazy even to go there?

No, her dream, fragile as the delicate stem of a rose, could only be a dream.

Carla lowered herself onto the window seat. She'd sit here and enjoy the morning…and wait for him to return.

As she sat watching, the plantation started to come alive. One by one, workers appeared, heading to different areas of the compound.

When she heard the sound of hoofs pounding the ground, Carla stood, anticipating Shayne's return. He soon came into her vision. Shayne was crouched over the horse's neck, appearing to be at one with the animal. Carla wished she had her camera. There was something breathtaking about the picture they created—they were perfection of motion.

When they reached the stables, the horse came to a sudden stop and Shayne dismounted in one fluid movement. Shayne patted the horse's head, and appeared to speak to it.

And then the most amazing thing happened; he placed his face in the horse's mane and nuzzled it gently.

In that moment, Carla Nevins fell hopelessly in love.

Chapter 5

That evening, as the sun cast its final light, Shayne watched Dr. Troy Whitehall drive down the driveway after his second checkup with Carla.

Finally deciding to face the inevitable, he mounted the stairs, heading to her room. When he knocked on the door, there was no immediate response. He knocked a second time.

"Come in." Her voice was soft and hesitant.

He entered, his gaze immediately finding her. She sat in the window seat, her eyes focused outside. She did not turn to acknowledge him, and he felt the strange sting of disappointment.

"I hope you enjoyed the meal Gladys brought you."

"Yes, it was very kind of her."

"I've instructed her to make sure you have anything you want. You just get the rest you need and I'll take care of everything else."

"Please, I don't want you to put yourself to any unnecessary trouble. I just came to let you know about the baby. It just seemed a bit too impersonal to call."

"I'm glad you did. Maybe when you're feeling a bit better, we can talk about the situation."

"I'm fine with that. I can only stay for the next few days. Then I must get back to Arlington."

"I know that was your original plan, but, under the circumstances, it may be better to stay here for a few weeks until you're feeling better."

"I'm not sure if that's a good idea." She kept her gaze down.

"Why?" he queried.

"I'm just not sure it is," she replied, but this time she looked up.

"Well, if that's the way you want it, I can't force you to stay. But I'll let you think about it and give me your answer later."

She nodded. "Okay, I promise I'll think about it."

"Good, that's all I ask. I have to go out for a

while, so you get some rest. I'll come see you later.
If there's anything you need, just call Gladys on the
intercom. She'll take care of you."

"Thank you. I appreciate everything you're doing."

"As I said before, it's not a problem. You're a
guest in my home."

"I'd like to make a call to my business partner
to let her know I may be staying a while."

"Sure. As I said, I want you to feel as comfortable as possible." He glanced at the suitcase,
which stood by the dresser. "Good, I see Lawrence
brought up your suitcases. I'm assuming you'll
stay here instead of going to the hotel."

"Yes, I'll stay."

"Good, that's the sensible thing to do. Troy—Dr.
Whitehall—wants to see you in a few days."

"He wants to see me? Is something wrong?" She
reached out and gripped his hand.

"No. He just wants to give you a regular checkup
and, since your little episode, I'd prefer it. I'll make
an appointment for Friday. I'll take you."

"You don't have to do that. I'm sure I can take
a taxi there once you give the driver the directions."

"Carla, let's get something straight right now so
that we don't have to deal with this each time the
situation arises. You're a guest in my home and I
expect you to let me treat you as I would treat any
guest in my house. The fact that you're pregnant

with my child gives me even more motivation to make sure that you have everything you need."

"Fine, I know when I'm outargued. However, as long as I stay here, I don't expect you or your staff to treat me like an invalid. I won't be treated as though I'm useless."

"I'll be sure to let them know of your wishes as long as you obey the doctor's instructions."

When she did not answer he smiled. *Good.* He hoped he'd get no more arguments from her.

"Gladys promised she'll bring dinner to you after you've rested. I was going to ask if you wanted dine with me downstairs, but your rest is more important. It will be better if Gladys brings your dinner to you. I had to make some last minute dinner plans, anyway."

"May I ask a question before you go?"

"Sure."

"Why did you leave the hotel that day?"

"There was a fire just on the other side of the plantation. A couple of families living there lost their homes. I had to make sure that they had somewhere to go. When I returned to the hotel, you were already gone."

"Are the families okay now?"

"Yes, they are. They have new homes and, when I checked yesterday, they were doing fine."

There was a knock at the door.

"Gladys, you may come in," Shayne said.

The housekeeper entered, carrying a well-laden tray, a broad smile on her face.

"Evening, Ms. Carla. I came to see how you were doing."

Carla smiled. "Thank you. I enjoyed the lunch you prepared for me," she said.

"It's a pleasure to have you here. I'm making Shayne's favorite for dinner, but he tells me he has a dinner engagement. I have a mind to put him over my lap and spank him."

Shayne responded with a loud, hearty laugh. "I think it's about time I take my leave. I'm sure your threat isn't an idle one and I don't want to be embarrassed in front of our guest."

Gladys responded with a stern look. "You go on to your dinner. I'll stay here and keep Ms. Carla company for a wee bit since you have more important things to do than to keep your guest company. You enjoy your dinner."

"Okay, Gladys, I promise I'll be in early, so no need to get antsy. Carla, I'll come by tonight if you're not asleep when I get here."

With that, he turned and left, closing the door gently behind him.

As he walked down the stairs he realized that he didn't want to leave. He wanted to be the one to spend time with Carla. He wanted to find that sexy, vibrant woman he'd met at the Hilton.

Instead, the woman who'd come to Barbados worried him with her fragility. She needed someone to take care of her and he had every intention of being that person.

When Shayne left the room, Carla felt a strange emptiness engulf her. An unexpected feeling. She wasn't even sure how to respond. Shayne Knight was affecting her a bit more than she wanted.

"Come, girly, you need to eat your dinner. I know he's a handsome man, but you have all the time to think 'bout him when I'm gone," Gladys said.

"I wasn't thinking about him," Carla responded vehemently.

"Of course you weren't." She paused for a moment. "But I should apologize. It was presumptuous to speak to you that way. We ain't accustomed to visitors and Shayne's like my son. It's a pity you ain't seen Russell. Girl, he's a heart-stopper. If you think Shayne's handsome, you should see his younger brother, Russell. That boy's going break 'nuff hearts when he's older."

"I'm sure his older brother has taught him well."

"So what's your plan? You and Shayne planning to get married?"

"I'm not sure about that. I have no plans to get married. I'm going to raise this child alone. I don't need anything."

"So Shayne don't have a say in this?"

"Yes, he does, that's why I came here to the island. I feel that any father has a right to know his child. But I'm not sure that Shayne wants to be a father."

"I think Shayne would be a good father. He may not feel so, right now, but I know how he was with his brother and sister when his parents died. He doesn't even realize he was their brother *and* their father for the past few years. He's had all the practice he needs."

"He has a sister as well as a brother?"

"Yes, but they're both overseas studying. Russell is in New York while Tamara is at university in Jamaica."

"How old are they now?

"They're both twenty-two. They're twins. So you never know, you might have twins, too."

"Twins?" She almost passed out thinking of the possibility.

"You don't worry, child. I'm going to go downstairs now and start on dinner. You take a rest, and I'll let you know when dinner is ready. I have to make sure you eat. You're carrying a Knight baby."

Carla decided against responding to Gladys's statement. She had intended to give her child her own last name. Giving her or him the Knight name would create a permanent bond between her baby and Shayne that she surely didn't want.

She'd discovered the Knight name was well-respected on the island. Shayne was successful and famous for agricultural research. She decided she needed to know more about the Knight family so that she could impart to her child his or her heritage some day.

"The Knights are a prominent family in this community, aren't they?"

"Yes, the family is a respected one." Gladys paused, this time placing her hands over her mouth. "See, you're going to make me talk more than I should. I'm preparing vegetable rice with baked ribs in a special sauce my mother taught me years ago. I hope you like to eat? But I'm going now. It's getting late and you need your rest."

Carla watched as Gladys left the room and then tried to stand. Her legs were a bit wobbly at first, but the slight trembling stopped and she walked cautiously over to the bathroom.

She brushed her teeth before she splashed water on her face. The face looking back at her was not an unpleasant one. She'd been told often enough she was attractive but, each time she caught a glimpse in the mirror, she wondered, what—if any—characteristics she possessed might cause a man's heart to beat faster.

She wondered if her unusual eyes could be an attraction, but knew that eyes alone could not attract a man. She did love her hair and loved the feel of it hitting just below her shoulders.

Her breasts were a bit too full for her slender frame, but pregnancy had a way of taking control of a woman's body, something she didn't particularly like.

Carla frowned. Her present vulnerability worried her. She definitely did not like the wraithlike image she saw in the mirror.

She hoped that after her stay in Barbados, Shayne's demand that she rest and Gladys's good food, she'd return to the fit, healthy woman she'd always been.

And, with a child on the way, she had to ensure that she was in the best condition.

Nothing must happen to this baby… Nothing.

Shayne entered the restaurant, his eyes scanning the dimly lit room. Immediately, a woman headed toward him, a genuine smile on her face.

"Mr. Knight, glad you could join us tonight. It's been a long time since you've visited our humble establishment."

"Jan, come off it. Come and give me a hug, girl. How's that hardworking husband of yours?"

"He's in the kitchen where he loves to be. One of the hostesses couldn't come in tonight, so I've stepped in to help out. It's good to get out of the kitchen sometimes. And Earl gets jealous when I create some of my fabulous dishes."

At his laugh, she smiled. "So, you're all alone tonight?"

"No. In fact, I'm meeting George here. We have some business to discuss. You know he uses our business talks just to get a free dinner here. He lets me know he's on the clock so I have to pick up the bill. Is he here yet?"

"No, but I can take you to your table. Dinner is on the house. I'll prepare George's favorite."

"Thanks, but I'll go to the bar and have a drink while I wait."

"Well, you know where it is. You must come to the house for dinner one night. We miss you."

"I've been really busy, but I promise to come over soon. I'll call."

Jan smiled that wide smile again and headed toward the entrance. A large group was just filtering in through the door.

Shayne headed to the well-stocked bar. Maybe, tonight he'd drink something stronger than the soda water, which he usually drank. He needed something to clear his head, but, immediately, he decided against quieting his nerves with hard liquor. He would have to focus on work this evening.

When his parents had passed away he'd taken to drinking, drowning his sorrows in the bottle, until one day Russell found him drunk and puking in his room. The look of disappointment and fear on his brother's face woke him up to the reality that he had two twelve-year-olds to take care of and that he was not the only one hurting. From that day on, he only drank socially, and that didn't happen often.

His current lapse in judgment was obvious.

He didn't like what she was doing to him.

He wasn't thinking rationally, anymore.

With each passing hour, Carla continued to ingrain herself in his mind. He just couldn't stop thinking about her.

She was an enigma.

Shayne remembered her passion during their time together. She'd been so intense, playing an equal role in their lovemaking. Again, he felt that telltale stir of arousal. Damn, he had to stop thinking about her, or he'd be walking around as hard and horny as a teenager.

Carla was a beautiful woman and he had responded to her beauty the moment he'd met her. When their eyes had connected, he'd seen the daring and promise in hers.

"Shayne, your usual?"

"You know me." He turned to the bartender. "And, of course, a gin and tonic for George." He nodded to his friend and lawyer who had just walked up to the bar.

"Of course. I need something a bit stronger to destress me, but right now, I'm too hungry to drink. Let's just go eat. I could eat a horse."

"George, I advised you not to tell jokes that involve eating horses. It gets me nervous whenever you come to visit. I'm expecting to see Mongoose disappear. And I'm still amazed at the amount that you can put away. Your appetite hasn't changed a bit since we left school."

"Shayne, let's not talk about me. This dinner is a business one, so as soon as we get to our table let's talk about business. What's wrong with you, anyway? Got some young woman pregnant?"

When Shayne didn't respond, George hesitated before he added. "I was just joking, bro. You don't have to look at me like I committed a crime. I know you haven't had a woman in ages, so that can't be it."

He went silent when there was no response again.

"You always had the knack for saying the craziest things," Shayne finally said. "This time what you said just happens to be true."

"Shayne, you got some woman pregnant?" George could not hide his shock.

"Yes," Shayne replied, realizing there was no sense in prolonging the inevitable.

"How? When? Where?"

"She's a little over four months pregnant and…"

"Four months pregnant and I'm just now finding this out? I'm supposed to be your best friend, Shayne. We tell each other everything. And I'm just now finding out I'm going to be a godfather?"

"Sorry, George. I only found out yesterday. I didn't know."

"Who is she? Where's she from? I hope it's not that girl who works at the gym. That's the only place you ever go."

"Remember when I stayed at the Hilton during the official opening in October, last year—when we had that cane fire? I met a woman from Arlington, Virginia, at the hotel and we spent a few days… I won't go into all the details, but, when I'd returned to the hotel a few days later, she was gone."

"And now she's pregnant? Where is she? Did she call?" Shayne almost laughed at the confusion on George's face.

"When I left home, she was in the guest room, sleeping."

"She's here?" When Shayne nodded in response, George continued. "She's after your money, right?"

"I don't think so. She owns her own travel agency in Arlington. So, no, I don't think so."

"So what's she doing here?" George asked.

"Told me she didn't want her child to grow up not knowing his or her father."

"A noble gesture, but you need to be careful. You need to be sure that she's all you believe her to be. I've had more experience with women than you, and this situation sounds real fishy to me. She may be dangling an apple right under your nose, but it could be a trap."

A flash of doubt flickered in Shayne's mind, but he immediately buried it.

"No, I'm convinced Carla is who she says she is. She hasn't asked for anything. All she wants is to let me know about the child. After that, I'm free to do what I want. I'll be happy to let her go back to the States. She can send the boy or girl to Barbados for the holidays. Her suggestions seem reasonable."

"And you're sure that's what you want to do? I'm not sure I'd want to give up a child so easily."

"I'm not giving the child up. I just don't want to be too involved in its life. I'm sure I won't make a good father."

"Shayne, I think you'd make a terrific father.

You were like a father to Russell and Tamara. What more proof could you want that you are daddy material?"

"Come on, George. Being a brother to two grown siblings is totally different from being a father. With Russell and Tamara, I didn't have a choice. Here, I have one, and the child would be much better off without me. I hardly have any time for myself and you want me to become a father? I'm sure the child would probably visit one summer and never want to return."

"You're hopeless. Let's not talk about this anymore. Our food is here. Tomorrow, you can give me a call and let me know what legal arrangements you want to support *your* child. I'll have the papers drawn up for you to sign as soon as possible."

"Good, that's what I'd hoped. I don't want to wait too long to take care of the financial aspect of this…situation. I'll call and tell you what I'm thinking would be a reasonable financial allowance."

"Fine with me. For now, I'm craving those baby back ribs that the waitress is going to set on my plate. This whole conversation has depressed me, and only eating will help."

"Ok, we'll eat, but there's some other plantation business I need to discuss with you."

"Good, and maybe I'll get the waitress to give me her number."

"Boy, I can see you have no intention of changing."

Before George could reply, the waitress arrived, placing their meals before them. With a smile, she politely refused to give George her number, informing him that she was happily married.

"All the good-looking ones are taken," George observed, as she walked away.

"George, under all that bravado and indifference, there's a lonely man looking for love just like all of us. Your time will come."

George laughed, a deep hollow sound. "Like your time has already come."

"Now, that's a crazy notion," Shayne scoffed.

No, his time had far from come. He definitely had no intention of getting hooked. Maybe, if Carla wasn't pregnant, he'd pick up where he'd left off, but the baby had definitely complicated matters.

Carla placed the spoon on the plate and sighed in contentment. The mango cheesecake had been truly sinful, and she hoped any weight she gained would put all the concerns she faced to rest. With Shayne gone, Gladys had asked her if she wanted to come downstairs for dinner.

Bored of the bedroom, despite how pretty it was, she'd agreed, allowing Gladys to lead her downstairs. At first, her knees had felt almost as if they would buckle under her weight, but by the time she reached the kitchen, she felt much better, despite the thin layer of sweat that covered her body.

Now, Carla sat alone. Gladys had retired to the kitchen to clean up, leaving her clear instructions that she shouldn't spend too much time watching television or reading since she should go to bed early and rest. Since her favorite show had been on television tonight and it was still early, she'd opted to do a bit of both. She'd watched the show and then browsed the shelf of books in the library.

An hour later, Carla stood in front of several shelves of books in a tiny room beyond the sitting room. Eagerly, she moved toward the closest shelf. She immediately spied a set of romance novels. The names of some of her favorite authors leapt out at her, and she pulled a copy of Brenda Jackson's latest from the shelf. She'd missed it when it had been released a few months ago, so she was delighted to get the opportunity to read it.

Content she would have a few hours of great reading, she turned to leave, but came to a stop when she noticed a picture on the large mahogany desk, which stood in a corner of the room.

Curious enough to take a closer look, she realized the photo was of Shayne and a young man and woman who she assumed were Russell and Tamara.

The girl was pretty, a wide smile on her lips, and

the eyes, which peered back were sharp and held the promise of intelligence. Her face was devoid of makeup, giving her a natural, healthy look.

The boy, definitely her twin, stared back, his gaze intense as if he rarely missed anything. He was not handsome like Shayne, but was beautiful in a masculine kind of way. Where Shayne was big and rugged and seemed born for the land, his brother carried a subtle cloak of academe.

Physically, the twins and Shayne were as different as day and night, but there were similarities in the slight tilt of their heads and the stubborn lines of their chins. And, of course, they all had startling black Knight eyes.

Carla remembered the first time she'd seen Shayne, the dark pools of his eyes had seemed fathomless. She had seen a spark of desire, but he'd allowed her to see very little of what lay beneath the surface.

Now, he was back in her life and nothing had changed. His eyes revealed only what he wanted her to see, and she wished he would let her inside. She wanted to unravel the mystery behind the man. She wondered what would have happened if she'd met him under difference circumstances. Shayne possessed all she found appealing in a man. Not only was he handsome and great in bed, he was a nice person.

What confused her most was his attitude toward

their unborn child. The air of indifference worried her, since her reason for being here was to ensure her child had a father as well as a mother.

Yes, she wanted custody of the child, but she wanted her child to know its family and, most of all, she wanted her baby to know its father.

For a man who'd raised two teenagers on his own, his attitude to fatherhood seemed strange. Gladys had told her all about the death of the elder Knights and the role Shayne had played in his sister and brother's lives.

Somehow, she knew he'd make a good father, but he seemed unable to see himself in that role.

Carla turned from the photo to head back down the corridor and upstairs to her room. She headed immediately to sit on the chair by the window, and flicked to the first page of the book she held in her hands. She couldn't wait to be transported into the world of romance and love.

Two hours later, she closed the book, a wide smile on her face.

That love scene was a bit too heated for her.

The hero had suddenly transformed himself into someone taller and darker, with eyes as black as midnight.

Whatever she tried to do, thoughts of Shayne intruded. As she'd read, she had been startled by the chemistry between the hero and heroine. Ironically, she seemed to be living her own story of passion, but she saw no happily ever after for her and Shayne.

Ten years from now, she'd probably be baking cupcakes for the latest PTA fundraiser and going home to a cold empty bed. A wave of dread washed over her and she realized that she did not want that for herself. She wanted more from life and, for the first time in years, a special man had stirred her enough for her to think of sharing her life with him.

Maybe she'd meet someone. She believed that everyone was destined to have a soul mate and, though she had no plans to marry again, she needed to think of the child growing inside her. Did she want her child to grow up without a father?

No. That's why she'd come to Barbados....

Well, only time would tell. Right now, she needed to rest and take things easy. The health of her baby was the most important thing and her baby's health depended on her.

Placing the book on the bedside stand, she stripped her clothes off and headed for the bathroom. Maybe a long hot shower would take the edge off her restless mind. She needed to focus less on Shayne Knight and forget her worries. Babies had a way of picking up these things, or so she'd heard.

But purging Shayne from her mind was easier said than done. As the water trickled down her body, Carla closed her eyes and inhaled the scent of Shayne's cologne lingering in the air. She inhaled deeply, feeling the warmth of his body next to hers. When she opened her eyes, she was alone; his body and touch were only a memory of another time, another place.

So the situation was proving to be a crazy one. Shayne and Carla were both being stubborn. Gladys realized that she'd been right about Carla and was growing to care about her. The two fools were falling in love with each other and didn't even realize it.

She admired Carla for making the decision to come to Barbados. She could easily have kept the child secret, but she had made the choice to let Shayne know that he was going to be a father.

What Gladys didn't like was their crazy plan!

A child needed a mother and a father. What nonsense was this about the child coming to Barbados for the summer? This was one time she was disappointed and angry with Shayne. She'd felt like knocking his head off when he'd told her his plan.

But she knew he wasn't thinking clearly. She knew he was scared. He would never admit it, but her boy was terrified to be a daddy. Not that he'd had the perfect example. Yeah, Charles Knight had loved his children, but he'd never had time for them. He was always working in the fields or cavorting with the woman.

Charles had thought Gladys knew nothing about his woman, that harlot, but she'd known. The idiot kept forgetting that Barbados was a small island and people loved to talk. The Dixon's maid had enjoyed telling her about Charles's affair with a woman from the village.

Fortunately, Charles had the sense to make sure there were no children. She could imagine the scandal on the island if anyone had discovered that Charles Knight had left an illegitimate child behind. She thanked God that Shayne, Russell and Tamara didn't have to deal with a situation like that.

Well, she'd watch how this situation played itself out. She had no doubt that Shayne would eventually do the right thing.

She'd already seen the cutest little pink dress in a tiny boutique on the south coast. It had baby Knight's name already written all over it....

Chapter 6

On Friday, Shayne stood naked by the window, remembering clearly the morning almost four months ago when he'd stood at this same spot contemplating what he should do with his life.

In the distance, he heard the familiar plantation sounds. But this morning, there were new sounds. Today heralded the beginning of the sugar-cane harvest. As the sugar industry had declined, he'd converted some of the fields into residential lots. Now only two-thirds of the plantation's arable land remained under sugar cane. The rest of the acreage was planted in lettuce, carrots and potatoes.

Harvesting of the cane crop would take about

four weeks. He hoped the weather would remain sunny and dry during the period. If the rains came too early, it would delay the harvest. A late-harvested crop was a sugar-cane planter's nightmare.

Before he headed out to the fields Shayne decided to inform Carla of the plans for later that day. Her appointment with Troy was scheduled for that evening.

Shayne glanced at the clock on the dresser, and went immediately to the bathroom. He emerged a few minutes later, feeling refreshed, but still needing a cup of coffee to get him going.

When he entered the kitchen, Gladys was there and a plate at his usual place was filled with scrambled eggs, bacon and a stack of toast.

"Morning, Gladys. You didn't have to get up so early. I told you I'd take care of my breakfast this morning."

"No problem, Shayne. I woke up early and couldn't get back to sleep. I was making breakfast for myself and decided to make yours at the same time. I'm sure your guest will sleep for a while. She needs all the rest she can get. That girl is too skinny. I can see she has been working herself too hard."

"So what do you expect me to do?" he asked, annoyed by her words. It seemed as if she wanted to blame him for Carla's condition.

"Do I have to tell you what to do? A woman is pregnant with your child and you ask me what to do?" Her voice rose, but Shayne could tell she was making an effort to control her anger.

"Gladys, I didn't ask for this. I was happy, content with my life. And now this."

"You should have thought of that before you unzipped your pants with a woman you didn't even know. You did ask for this, so I'm going to let you know how I feel. Don't know what's happening to you all of a sudden. You've always acted so responsibly. At least, the woman you slept with is a decent woman. At least, you've learned a bit of what I've been trying to teach you all these years."

With that, she slammed the frying pan she held in her hand on the counter, gave him the look that told him she was more than disappointed with him and walked out in a huff.

A four-letter word he didn't usually use almost slipped from his lips. He'd messed up royally by saying things he shouldn't, but he wanted to appear unperturbed by this situation, which threatened to drive him over the brink. Revealing how he felt would only make him more vulnerable.

For a while, Shayne sat there, a story from his childhood vivid in his mind. He remembered his mother telling him the story of a knight who did all he could to save and help others. As a child, he'd dreamed of being that chivalrous defender of people in need. To some extent, he'd become that person, making contributions to worthy organizations on the island.

But what scared Shayne most about being this noble person, was that he might expose too much of his gentler side to those around him. He didn't want people to see him in this light. People knew him as the strong, no-nonsense plantation owner, Shayne Knight. He'd fought long and hard to establish his reputation, especially in a business that, historically, had been controlled by the whites on the island. He had no intention of losing the respect he'd gained by being perceived as soft.

He may be a big marshmallow on the inside, but he didn't have any intention of letting everyone know it.

The sound of footsteps forced him to turn, and Gladys entered the room.

"Shayne, forgive me for what I just said. I didn't mean to snap. I'm sorry I disrespected you."

"Gladys, you don't need to apologize. You've earned the right to tell me when I've been foolish. Come here and give me a hug."

She came to him and, when he placed his arms around her, he felt that familiar comfort. Her head rested on his shoulder.

Gladys was more than just the housekeeper, she

was family. She'd remained with him when his parents had passed away, offered help with Russell and Tamara without reservation. She'd become a mother and a friend to each of them. Shayne could remember the times when she'd helped him to deal with a particularly frustrating situation with his younger siblings.

"Come, you get off to work. I'll finish breakfast for your guest. I heard her stirring when I passed her room a few minutes ago."

"Thanks for taking care of her."

"I like her. She is a very pleasant individual. Now, you take your arms from around me and get on to work."

They both turned at the sound of footsteps coming down the hallway, pulling instinctively apart.

Seconds later, Carla entered, and Shayne's heart stopped for the briefest of moments before it restarted at a rapid rate.

Carla was lovely. Simply dressed in a pair of jeans and a close-fitting white blouse, she stood poised at the door, a look of uncertainty on her face as she looked at him.

When she turned to Gladys, she smiled, her eyes soft and warm.

Gladys, already busy at the stove, said, "Carla, please have a seat at the table. I'll soon have your breakfast ready."

"Thank you," Carla replied.

"I hope you eat pancakes. I'm going to make you my special Bajan pancakes."

"I do, but please don't put yourself to any trouble."

"Girl, you going to let me do my work? I'm going to give you the fluffiest pancakes you've ever tasted." She turned to Shayne. "You still there? You not going to work, anymore?" Shayne heard the laughter in her voice. It was definitely time for him to go.

"Yes, I'm going now. Carla, I'll come back this afternoon. Your appointment for the ultrsound's at two-thirty."

"Thank you. I'll be ready," Carla replied.

"Okay, ladies, I'll say bye, for now. I have a meeting in Bridgetown this morning. Don't worry about me for lunch. I'll have something downtown, because I also have to go see George."

Reluctantly, he turned and left the room, refusing to look back. He knew he'd probably want to stay and have breakfast with Carla if he hesitated.

When she'd arrived, Shayne's focus had been all about his concern for her. Yes, he was still concerned, but this morning, he was reminded of how beautiful she was. Just seeing her had an electrifying effect on him.

Outside, he quickly retrieved his vehicle from

the garage and was soon speeding south to Bridge-town.

Shayne loved it here in St. Thomas, one of two landlocked parishes on the island. The other nine parishes all boasted white sand beaches on the Atlantic or the Caribbean oceans.

As he drove, the ocean breeze cooled the heat of the tropical sun, so he didn't turn the air-conditioning on. In any case, he preferred the freshness of the open air.

Flicking his cell open, Shayne used the automatic dial command to call George to inform him he'd be at his office just after midday. Leaving his message with the answering service, Shayne returned his focus to the road ahead.

Ten minutes later, despite the thick stream of traffic, he arrived in the city, parked his car in the usual spot and headed for his meeting, trying, without success, to put the image of Carla from his mind.

Carla exited the house and headed in the direction of the swimming pool Gladys had pointed out to her. She needed to relax and a short swim in the pool and an hour or two reading would be the perfect way to spend the rest of her morning, before she got ready for her appointment.

The water from the pool glistened, beckoning

her with its coolness. She enjoyed swimming. Her short stint on her high-school swim team had been one of the highlights of her years in school. She'd not been the competitive type and had soon joined the photography club.

Placing her robe on one of the lounge chairs lining the pool, she moved to stand at its edge and then expertly slipped into the water, knowing that a dive was out of the question.

When she pulled herself from the pool half an hour later, her body felt good. She'd swum quite a few laps before switching onto her back to look up at the dancing clouds above.

Lying on a towel on the lounge chair under a large umbrella, she quickly found the page where she'd placed a piece of paper and was soon absorbed in the story.

What she wouldn't do to meet a real man like the hero in the romance novel she was reading.

Shayne immediately came to mind. He was as yummy as any romance hero. Rich, handsome, strong and confident, he appeared the typical alpha male, but, at times, she caught a glimpse of his gentler side. The way he'd looked at her when she'd awakened and found him in her room. The lowering of his voice when he'd talked about his brother and sister and the genuine affection she saw when he looked at Gladys.

Somewhere inside, there was a gentleness of spirit she wanted to see more of and experience. She wanted to get to know the gentle side of this man.

Her last thought before she fell asleep was the reality that she was carrying his child.

When Shayne arrived home just after midday, he immediately headed for the sitting room where he knew Gladys would be watching her favorite soap opera.

"Is Carla in her room?" he asked, trying to keep his voice as natural as possible. He felt somewhat disappointed that Carla wasn't in the parlor with Gladys.

"No, she's out by the pool," Gladys said, without taking her eyes from the television program. "She's wearing a red swimsuit and she took a book with her. I thought she'd be back by now. Why don't you go check on her and let me finish watching my story?"

"I'll go get her."

"Lunch is already prepared so she can eat when she wants to. You can have some of the pasta and tossed salad, too."

"Thanks, I was hoping you'd made enough for me to have some. George had an important meeting with a client, so he cancelled on me. But he did say he'll be over to dinner one night this week."

"That'll be great. I haven't seen him over for a while."

"He's been busy working on a murder trial, but he'll be over soon. He can't resist your cooking." He bent over and kissed her on the forehead. "So whose brother is sleeping with whose brother's wife?" His laughter echoed in the room as he left.

He took the shortest route to the pool, preferring to take the exit through the kitchen. He was pretty proud of the twenty-five-foot pool he'd had built a few years ago when Tamara had decided to take up competitive swimming. With the island's aquatic centre several miles away, he'd built the pool as an alternative training site for her.

In the distance, he could see Carla lying on one of the chairs dotting the circumference of the pool.

When Shayne reached her, he realized she was sleeping, an open novel resting on her stomach.

Her softly swollen stomach.

His child.

He wondered if the baby would be a girl or boy.

Shayne looked down at Carla and realized that, even in sleep, Carla's beauty stole his breath. He'd always found pregnant woman physically unattractive, but seeing Carla like this, swollen with his child, made him realize that in pregnancy a woman was at her most beautiful.

Shayne felt the urge to touch her stomach. He

wanted to feel his child, but he didn't want to do it without her permission.

He resisted the temptation. It wouldn't matter anyway. He didn't intend to be too much a part of her life after she bore his child.

Though George had tried to convince him that he was being silly about the situation, he had no intentions of changing his mind. He preferred to be a summer dad, if there was such a thing. The child would come to Barbados for three or four weeks in July or August and then return to his mother in the United States.

To him, it seemed a very reasonable arrangement. Of course, the arrangement would depend on Carla's agreement. He would send her a generous monthly allowance and make sure the child had the best education possible.

Shayne felt proud of himself. He was being responsible, so no one would complain. Not even Gladys.

"Carla," he said, shaking her gently.

She stirred, her chest rising, allowing him full view of her breasts. He felt the familiar stir of his arousal. Damn, she was turning him into a pervert, but he couldn't help it. He had no doubt that he'd soon have to take matters into his own hands if this situation did not correct itself. Carla seemed to have awakened his long-buried sexual drive.

"Carla," he said again, louder.

Her eyes finally opened, slowly, widening with alarm when she realized he stood over her. She sat upright, reaching immediately for her robe and placed it around her.

"You're back, already? What time is it?"

"It's just after noon. You have some time. I got my business completed earlier than I expected. Gladys says lunch is ready, so we can go eat and then you can get ready for the doctor."

"I prefer to take a shower first. I'll be down as soon as I'm done."

They walked back to the house, a wall of silence between the two of them. Shayne felt the need to say something, but he couldn't find the right words. When they reached the stairs, she smiled politely and told him she would be ready soon. Shayne headed for the kitchen.

In the kitchen, he worked quickly. He warmed the pasta and placed the bowl of salad onto the table. He took a pitcher of lemonade from the refrigerator, found two glasses and also placed them on the table.

He knew the polite thing to do was to wait, but the rumble in his stomach told him that he was hungrier than he'd realized.

Sitting, he spooned generous portions of the pasta and salad onto a plate and proceeded to eat.

His taste buds tingled with pleasure. He could never understand how Gladys could take the most mundane ingredients and make something special out of them. Add the best-tasting lemonade in the world and he knew why eating at home was a must. He only ate out when business necessitated he do so.

Unlike Russell and Tamara, who'd frequently helped Gladys in the kitchen, he'd been too busy trying to keep the home and the business together to learn to cook. One day, he planned to rectify that situation.

But he had every intention of keeping Gladys around forever. If he did eventually get married, his wife would have to accept that he came with a housekeeper.

He returned his attention to the meal just as Carla entered the room. As expected, his heart stopped. She was a ray of sunshine in a yellow, loose-fitting dress, which did little to hide her pregnancy, but emphasized the glow of impending motherhood.

She stood quietly before him when she reached the table.

"I've set a place for you, you can sit here," he said, standing to pull a chair out for her.

"What a gentleman," she said, smiling her thanks, before she sat.

"Yeah, Gladys taught me well," he responded, returning to his chair. "She'd knock my head off if I didn't uphold the law of etiquette and I try not to get on her wrong side."

"You love her a lot, don't you?" she asked, spooning some of the pasta and salad onto her plate.

"Yes, she was here for us—Tamara, Russell and me—when our parents died. I don't know what I would have done if she hadn't been here. Imagine a twenty-two-year-old inheriting a large plantation and having to become father to twelve-year-old twins."

"Well, you must have done it, since you seem to have been very successful with the plantation. I know most of the plantations on the island have stopped growing sugar cane since tourism has taken over as the main industry. And the fact that your brother and sister have both gone off to university suggests that you did a pretty good job with them, too."

"I don't think I've done too badly. They've turned out to be good kids. Not that it was always easy, but, for the most part, they have made sensible choices."

"You must be proud of them."

"I'm definitely proud of the young adults they have become. There isn't a prouder brother anywhere in the world. But too much talking. I'm stopping you from eating."

"I am a bit hungry. The exercise in the pool was great. I did about thirty laps."

"Thirty laps? Impressive, but remember you're supposed to take things easy."

"I took my time and didn't exert myself. Thirty laps is way below my usual amount. I wasn't on the varsity swim team for nothing."

"No wonder you have that perfectly toned figure."

"Thanks for the compliment, but I'm not sure I can be called 'perfectly toned' right now. I'm swelling like an elephant. Of course, I'll be back to my regular fitness routine once he's born."

"He?"

"Yes, I'm convinced he's a boy."

"Yeah?"

"Oh, we women know these things. He'll look just like you, too," she said, her voice laced with humor.

He laughed, laying his fork on the plate. "Ah, that was delicious. I'm going to leave you and go upstairs to take a shower. You can eat in peace. I'll be down in about fifteen minutes."

Shayne walked to the sink, washed the few things in there and headed to his room. Glancing at her, he smiled before he left the kitchen.

In his room, he quickly stripped and entered the shower. Turning the faucet to cold, he stayed under the water for as long as he could, allowing its chill to cool the raging fire inside his body. Just being around Carla, whatever time of the day, aroused the same response in him.

Shayne wished she were here with him now. The first time they'd attempted to take a shower, they'd made love several times before actually bathing. That sure had been fun. There'd been something exciting and highly erotic about making fast, heated love with water cascading on them.

When they'd both climaxed, he'd started kissing her all over, only to realize his erection had returned fast and furious. Without hesitation he'd entered her again, this time taking her with a slow gentle pace. They'd returned to the bed, made love again and had eventually fallen asleep. The shower had been forgotten until the next morning.

Forcing himself from the vivid memory, he finished his shower, dressed quickly and headed downstairs. He only stopped long enough to tell Gladys they would be leaving shortly.

When he reached the kitchen, Carla was drying the plates and glasses they'd used.

"You could have left those. Gladys would do them."

"No problem. I'm done. It didn't hurt to wash them."

"I just don't want you to think you have to do that stuff," he said. "Ready to go?"

"Just need to go upstairs and get my handbag."

"Cool, meet me out front. I'll get the car from the garage."

He watched as she left the room, her hips swaying from side to side.

He wondered how was he going to get through the afternoon.

Upstairs, Carla quickly brushed her teeth, squirted herself with her favorite fragrance and headed downstairs. Passing the sitting room, she stopped to tell Gladys goodbye, but the housekeeper was gone. Her soaps must be over.

Shayne was already parked at the front entrance when she exited the house, the car purring softly. Shayne stood by the passenger's side and opened the door as she drew near. She lowered herself into the seat, locking the seatbelt around her, and waited until Shayne took his seat, and they pulled away from the house.

For several minutes, they traveled in silence. Carla watched the passing scenery, preferring not to focus on the man sitting next to her. Her attraction to him never failed to unsettle her. This morning he'd been dressed in a casual navy-blue blazer, a pale-blue shirt and gray trousers. This afternoon, he wore a close-fitting pair of jeans and a knit shirt, which hugged his body, emphasizing his bulging muscles. She could tell he was fit. It was obvious that, even though he owned the plantation, he didn't leave all the manual work to his employees. He often worked alongside them. Gladys had told her that much.

Shayne's voice interrupted her musing. "So, did you enjoy your swim?"

"Yes, I did. You have a nice pool."

"I would have joined you if I'd had time, but I'll be sure to join you next time. I try to use the pool as often as I can, but I prefer to ride. And things have been hectic on the plantation with the harvest almost in full swing."

"I'm sorry to hear that I've only added to your stress."

"Never, ever think that, Carla. I can handle the pressure. You did the right thing to tell me about the child. I would have wanted to know."

"I'm glad I did. I couldn't deny you knowing your child. It would have been wrong. At least, I know I've done the right thing. What you decide to do now is all up to you. My conscience is clear." Shayne heard the determination and conviction in her voice.

"Carla, I need to be honest with you," he replied. "I'm not sure what part I will play in all this. Am I ready to be a father? I'm not sure. If I were to answer now, it'd more likely be no. I'm not ready. Can I love this child? Yes, I think so. Do I want to be a father? Again, the answer would have to be no. However, I do know that I'll be there for you. I'll make sure you get the best care possible and I'll make sure you're provided for. But the other things? I'm just not sure."

"Thanks for your honesty, Shayne. That's all I want. I have no doubt that you will make a wonderful father. But time will take care of that."

When Shayne glanced at her, she was not surprised at his cynical look and, in that moment, she realized something: Shayne was afraid. Afraid to be a father to the child growing inside her. And she ached for him, the boy who'd been forced to grow up too early, the boy who'd been forced to be father, mother and brother.

She glanced across at him, noticing the strength in the curve of his chin, the proud tilt of his nose. She knew, beyond a shadow of doubt, that he was a good man.

She would make sure her son or daughter knew him as their father.

"Like what you see?" he whispered, his voice husky with desire.

"What are you talking about?"

"You're staring at me like I'm something to eat," he responded.

"I wasn't," she denied, turning to stare out the window.

"If you insist. But I can tell this…thing between us isn't over. You want me as much as I want you."

She turned back to glare at him. "What? You're mighty presumptuous. I feel nothing for you." She knew he didn't believe her, but she said it anyway.

"Is that so? Maybe I should put it to the test," he challenged.

"Test?" she asked, knowing exactly what he meant, but she pretended not to understand.

"Yes, test. Maybe I should show you what still exists between us. I still want you. Every time I come close to you, I still see you lying in my arms, pleasuring me in the most intimate way. If you can honestly say that you don't want me, I'll leave you alone."

"I'd be grateful if you would. I came to let you know about the child, but I had no plans of ending up in your bed. This is strictly about the baby."

"Okay, if that's your final word. I assure you, I won't come begging. However, we'll have to continue this conversation at a later date. We've arrived at Troy's office."

The car stopped outside a building, which looked more like a home than a doctor's office. Shayne stepped out and came to the passenger's side to let her out.

Before entering the house, he turned to her.

"No need to be worried, Carla. Everything is going to be fine."

When he took her hand, Shayne noticed she was trembling. He squeezed it, trying to reassure her.

And they walked into the building.

An hour later, they were driving away. Carla noticed that the look on Shayne's face reflected hers.

She was worried, too. The doctor had emphasized, again, the importance of her taking things easy. The baby was doing well, but her blood pressure was elevated. She couldn't do anything that would be detrimental or cause complications. Her baby was also a bit smaller than it should be at this stage of the pregnancy.

She was having a little boy.

Her little boy.

She felt the sting of tears.

"Carla, don't cry. We'll take things easy. I'll do everything in my power to make sure nothing goes wrong."

The car pulled off the main road. They arrived at a quiet beach area dotted with park benches. Shayne parked the car in a small parking area, slipped from the car and opened her door.

"Come, let's sit here for a while. This is one of my favorite spots. I always come here when I just need to relax and unwind."

He led her to one of the benches, waiting until she sat before he joined her.

The sea sparkled in the distance, the bright sunlight making the day clear. The beach was almost devoid of swimmers, only a few tourists lying on large beach towels enduring the blistering heat to gain that perfect tan that one couldn't get out of a bottle.

"I can see why you love to sit here. It's beautiful."

"Yes, the first time I came here was the day my parents died. I'd just come from the hospital. Gladys was taking care of the twins, and I just couldn't go home. I couldn't face them. I didn't know how to tell them about Mom and Dad. I was passing by, saw this quiet spot and stopped. Of course, it's been renovated over the years, but I still come here whenever I'm dealing with a difficult problem." He paused. "I'm sure you think I'm crazy."

"No, I don't. I'm sure we all find comfort in some things, some places. Me, I just locked myself in my room and turned the lights off. That's the only way I could get peace and quiet when I was in foster care. Some things just become a part of us." She paused for a moment. "Thanks for sharing this place with me."

"You know the craziest thing happened this evening when we were at the doctor's. Before we went there I just saw the baby as a baby. Now that I know the baby's a boy, things feel different. Am I making sense to you?"

"Yeah, I feel the same way."

For a moment, they were silent and then she said what was foremost on her mind.

"Shayne, I'm scared. I don't want to lose this baby. I want him so badly, I can almost imagine holding him, hearing him cry at night when he's hungry," she paused, her anguish evident. "I don't want to lose him."

"You won't, Carla. I'm going to make sure nothing goes wrong."

When the tears started to fall, she drew closer to him, immediately feeling the strength of his arms around her.

Hours later, when the sun turned the color of the sky from brilliant red to pale orange, he held her hand and led her back to the car.

Something had happened between them as they'd sat and talked. Something had changed. Their relationship had taken a step in another direction.

He had to be careful, or he'd find himself losing his heart to Carla. He didn't want to admit it, but he sensed that he was falling in love with her.

Chapter 7

Carla watched as the credits of one of her favorite movies scrolled up the large plasma screen. Of course, the skill of Halle Berry and Jessica Lange's performance in *Losing Isaiah* only made the movie's poignant message more forceful.

Not that she had any intentions of giving her child, her son, away.

Her son.

She smiled, a warmth stirring deep in her heart. Already, she felt a profound love for the child growing inside her. Again, she wondered who the child would look most like.

Shayne?

Her?

Of course, she wouldn't know for another few months, but it really didn't matter. Either way, she'd have a beautiful son.

Someone to love.

Carla pressed the volume button on the remote control to lower the sound of the television. Now that the movie was over, maybe she'd get some sleep. Her body felt tired and she needed the rest. She'd tossed and turned for hours, bombarded by the words of the doctor. She couldn't lose her son, but even this state of sleeplessness could be aggravating the problem.

She stood, moving toward the window, but changed her mind, going back to the bed. She needed to sleep. She flicked the television off, pulled the covers over her and closed her eyes.

Thirty minutes later, Carla opened her eyes. Sleep was nowhere near touching her eyelids.

She climbed out of bed again and headed for the window seat. Maybe a few minutes of the cool night breeze would lull her to sleep.

She took a few cautious steps, her eyes adjusting to the darkness.

Suddenly, Carla found herself flying through the air, her feet off the ground. She screamed as she stretched her hands out, trying to break the fall. When she landed, however, she felt her hands twist under her and she felt a sharp pain flash through her head.

For what seemed like hours, she lay there, her breathing broken and ragged. She moved her hand from its awkward position beneath her body. It hurt a bit, but it did not appear broken. She wiggled her legs and they too seemed unbroken.

About to attempt to stand, she heard a knock at her door.

"Carla, is everything all right? I heard a scream." It was Shayne. She knew he'd come.

She tried to answer, but she could make no sound.

Before she knew it, the door flew open and Shayne entered, the light from the hallway created a dull aura around him.

He moved quickly to where she lay, bending to draw closer to her.

His hands probed her body, gently. "What happened?" he asked.

"I don't know. One minute I was headed to the window and the next thing I know, I'm on the ground."

He reached beneath her, lifting her in his arms with ease and laid her on the bed with the utmost care.

"You don't seem to have broken anything. Is it hurting anywhere? Your head? Arms?"

"No, I'll be fine. My hands broke the fall so I'm fine. I just feel a bit sore and battered. My head hurts a little."

"I'll go downstairs and get a glass of water and some pain medicine for the headache. Stay in bed and don't move!"

About to shout "Yes, sir," she decided against it. She'd done enough for the night. Instead, she gave him a polite "Thank you" and closed her eyes. The slight pain in her head began to throb steadily.

When he returned a few minutes later, she'd finally almost drifted off to sleep.

Shayne turned the lights on and stood over her, rousing her. She noticed he was wearing a pair of pajama pants instead of the boxers he'd worn when he'd entered before. Now, she could see his lean upper body and the six-pack abdominals. She averted her eyes, trying to stem the reaction she knew was coming.

Shayne walked toward her, concern on his face.

"Come, drink some water and take these two tablets for your headache. I'll ask Troy to drop by in the morning before he goes in to work," he said, handing her the glass.

"Thank you," she replied, taking the glass and downing the tablets. "There's no need to call the doctor. I'll be fine."

"Remember, you have a baby to think about now. You had a fall tonight that may not seem serious but, after what Troy said today, we have to be careful. I don't want anything to happen to you or the baby."

"If you insist," she replied. "I think I'll try to get some sleep now."

"You do that. I'll sit here and wait until you fall asleep."

"Okay," she said.

He'd not expected her to agree so easily.

He took the glass from her and rose to turn the light off, before returning to sit in the chair next to her bed.

"Shayne?" Her voice was the faintest of whispers.

"Yes."

"You want to lie next to me? I don't want to be here all by myself."

"Okay," he said. He stood and got into the bed with her, pulling the covers over them.

"Thanks," she said.

"No problem. Anything to please a guest."

She said nothing in response. Instead, she drew closer to him.

For a while, he lay there, her closeness assaulting all of his senses. Her steady breathing made him aware that she was sleeping. She shifted again, moving even closer, her arms resting on him. He, too, shifted to a more comfortable position and became aware of her breasts pressed against his chest.

Well, she was asleep, but he knew there would be no sleep for him.

In the morning, he would call Troy. He'd definitely feel better if his friend took a look at her. If this was what he had to deal with over the next few months, his life was going to change drastically. But it was his duty to take care of her and the baby.

He knew it was more than that. Carla was much more than his duty. She was the mother of his child, his son, and he had no intention of letting anything happen to either of them.

Shayne drew closer to her, placing his arms around her. She snuggled closer. Damn, she felt good. He could do this every night.

His last thought before he fell asleep was that, somehow, Carla had worked herself into his heart.

When Carla opened her eyes the next morning her immediate reaction to the body lying next to her was to scream as loudly as she could. Then she realized that Shayne was the man lying next to her.

She shifted, becoming aware of his firm length pressed against her. As her mind cleared of the fog of sleep she remembered that she'd asked him to spend the night with her. What had possessed her to ask him? At least, his sleeping next to her had helped. She'd slept through the rest of the night.

For a while, she lay there basking in the warmth of his body. He stirred, drawing closer to her, his arms wrapped around her. She was reminded of

their time together at the Hilton. Though they'd
spent little of it sleeping, she remembered this
much about that time: Despite not knowing each
other well, there'd been a comfortable intimacy
between them. They'd hugged and kissed and cuddled. They'd had very little talk, but they had
reached out to each other until she knew his body
in the intimate way that only lovers can.

She'd only been given a brief glimpse into the
person he was. She'd seen the fire in his eyes and
felt the tenderness in the touch of his hands and
the passion in every stroke of his body against her.
She'd enjoyed every moment of the sexual contact
between them and had played an equal part in all
that had taken place.

Now her body tingled with the memory and she
willed herself to get up. Before she could, she felt
Shayne's hand caressing her chin drawing her head
up to look into the dark pools of his eyes. His eyes
were alert and she realized that he must have been
awake for a while. When she felt the sudden jerk
of his erection, she almost came undone.

When his lips found hers, she wrapped her arms
around him, pressing herself against him. She
didn't know if it was safe but she wanted to feel
him inside her.

The kiss deepened, and she felt her bones melt
with the heat between them.

"I don't know what magic you're working on me, Carla, but I do know I want you now."

He raised her, pulling her gown from her. Then she watched as he lowered his pajama bottoms and tossed them to the floor. His penis sprang free, causing her heart to race even faster.

When he came to her, she instinctively opened her legs, welcoming him into her willing warmth. His entry was hard and firm and she flung her head back with the joy of feeling every inch of him inside her. She wrapped her legs around him tightly, drawing him closer. Inside her, his penis jerked, causing her to shiver. He started to move, but she stopped him.

"Not yet. I just wanted to enjoy this moment. I've felt so empty, I need to feel you."

For a while, they lay there until she tightened her muscles, letting him know she was ready.

"I'll be slow. I don't want to hurt you."

"Yes, take it slow. I want to enjoy this," she said.

He took her with a slow leisurely rhythm that made her want to scream with each stroke.

Soon, she joined him, allowing her body to meet him halfway. As she moved, she clenched her inner muscles, gripping his penis until beads of sweat appeared on his body and he groaned her name.

When she felt that telltale increase in movement and the periodic shudder in his body, she knew his climax was near and she deliberately eased the pace, taking control and prolonging his pleasure.

She enjoyed the control, but then things changed and her own body sparked with an intense heat. The passion built until she realized her release was also near.

She felt it coming from deep within, the sweet pain of pleasure, until she could take no more. Aware that he had reached his climax, she joined him, her own body convulsing in intensity.

Exhausted, she enjoyed the feel of his body on hers.

For a while they lay holding each other, tasting each other with light tender kisses.

"Come, let's take a shower. It's still too early in the morning to get up, but I prefer to bathe when the water is still cool."

He slipped from the bed, helping her up and leading her to the bathroom. He turned the shower on, ensuring the water was just warm enough before pointing the nozzle toward her.

Carla felt the urge to kiss him, but, instead, reached for his penis and, gripping it firmly, experienced a sense of power when it grew firm and thick in her hand. She caressed him gently, loving the way his body trembled with pleasure.

"I want you again," he groaned, the strangled sound emphasizing his restraint.

"So what are you waiting for?" she asked. She wanted him, too.

Shayne placed her back against the cool wall, capturing her lips with his. He tasted her, enjoying the soft sweetness she so willingly offered.

Placing his hand behind her to cup her buttocks, he entered her in one swift movement, groaning with the feel of her around him.

Their mating lacked the tenderness of before, but this time, they both gave in to their primitive instincts. For a moment, their eyes locked and he saw the wild passion in her eyes.

With each stroke, the heat intensified, and she responded with cries that only served to arouse him even more.

When she closed her eyes, he knew she was near to coming. And then he, too, felt the rumble of release and he wanted them to come together in body and mind.

Moments later, his body tensed and every nerve came alive and he, once again, experienced release. At the same time, Carla screamed, gripping him tightly until he felt that he would fall to the floor.

Satiated, he breathed deeply and his lips sought hers. As the water cascaded on their bodies and he felt the familiar stir of arousal, he realized he wanted her again.

* * *

When Carla woke in the morning, Shayne was gone. She stretched with contentment, her body tingling in evidence of their lovemaking. Something had happened last night. Her response to him had been different, more intense. Previously, their contact had been all about the excitement and daring, but now she'd caught a glimpse of something else, something strange and gentle. She'd caught a glimpse of the real Shayne's capacity to love.

No words had been spoken between them. There had been no need for any. His touch had been enough to create the music that flowed from him to her.

Carla rose from bed and headed immediately for the bathroom, stopping in her tracks when she noticed a piece of paper on the desk in the right-hand corner of the room.

She picked it up and read the brief note.

I'll be at work for most of the day. Troy will pass by to see you. Get some rest.
Shayne.

She smiled. Yes, she definitely needed the rest. Neither of them had slept much during the night. She hoped that the excessive exercise wasn't going much against the doctor's order, especially since she'd taken that fall. Troy had embarrassed them when he'd told them they could have a normal sex life. But he'd emphasized the need to take it easy. Last night, they hadn't taken it easy. They'd gone all-out.

However, Shayne had been gentle, taking care that she didn't overexert herself, but she'd wanted to be a part of their coming together as much as he had been.

In the light of the morning, she wondered if she'd made the worst mistake of her life, but as she stood in the shower, she realized that being here in Barbados was about more than just the child she carried. She could now admit that part of this journey was to discover if her feelings for Shayne were more than mere sexual attraction. And she hoped that he felt something for her, too.

Last night had provided evidence that their feelings for each other went much deeper than sex. She'd realized it in the gentle touch of his hand, his care and concern when he'd taken her. She'd seen his stark vulnerability when he'd cried out her name in the throes of passion.

She loved Shayne Knight and her body sang with the joy of the knowledge. Her feelings didn't surprise her. She knew she had feelings for him from the day she'd watched him with his horse. That day he had revealed a softer side of himself.

Turning the shower off, Carla quickly dried and

dressed, wondering how best to pass the day without boring herself to death.

She moved to the window overlooking the courtyard, closed her eyes and inhaled deeply, the tropical breeze startling her with its warmth.

In the midst of her musings, she heard a sound. Someone was knocking on her door. She sighed, unsure about facing Gladys. She hoped the elderly woman was unaware of what had taken place in her room the night before.

When she opened the door, as she'd anticipated, Gladys stood there, a smile on her face.

"Dr. Troy is here to see you. Says Shayne asked him to come over. Of course, I know he's only using this as an opportunity to get a good breakfast."

Carla chuckled at Gladys's words. "The visit's fine with me."

"Good, I'll let him come up in a few minutes."

"Of course, invite him to come right up," Carla said.

Gladys turned to leave, but not before Carla noticed the telltale twinkle in her eyes. Carla felt her cheeks warm with the heat of embarrassment. Gladys knew about last night!

Well, Carla had no one to blame but herself. She was the one who'd screamed her head off. What was happening to her? Just the touch of Shayne's hands turned her into a common cliché, she was putty in his hands.

She glanced at herself in the mirror before she sat on the small sofa next to the bed.

There was a knock on the door and then it swung open. Troy entered, his usual pleasant smile in place. Like Gladys, however, his eyes carried a knowing twinkle.

"So, how're you doing this morning, Carla?"

"I'm fine. Shayne is just being a bit overprotective."

"It's understandable. Men are like that. We tend to want to protect what belongs to us."

"But I don't belong to him," she said, hesitating a bit before she continued. "I may be carrying his child, but I've been taking care of myself for years."

"I'm not questioning your ability to take care of yourself. I'm just saying that Shayne now feels a responsibility to take care of you…and the baby."

"I guess I can understand. I'm assuming this is some kind of macho ego thing that men feel obliged to display. However, I will make it clear that I'm quite capable of taking care of myself and my child."

"Well, that's something that you and Shayne will have to discuss. I'm just the doctor. I did tell you yesterday that you could continue with regular sexual activity, but you needed to take things easy.

All-night sex may not be advisable. I've already spoken to Shayne this morning."

When she blushed, Carla realized that Troy's smile seemed a bit wider. "You did?"

"Yes, he did call this morning about some concerns he had, so I gave him the same advice I'm giving you."

At a loss for words, Carla just nodded her head. She felt as if she would sink into the floor and then she realized she was being silly. Finally, she said, "It seems that it makes no sense for me to be embarrassed. Shayne has spoken to you. I'll make sure we discuss things this evening when he gets home." She tried to keep the anger from her voice, but Troy's response told her she'd not been successful.

"Come on, Carla, I'm your doctor, there's no need to be angry with Shayne and you don't have to be embarrassed about anything. You have to understand that Shayne is accustomed to caring for the people he loves. You're safe with him."

When she didn't respond he said, "Good, I need to take a quick listen to that boy of yours. Let's see how he's doing."

Ten minutes later, Troy took his gloves off and slipped them into his bag.

"Well, Carla, you're doing fine today. Just a small bruise on your hand, no evidence of a concussion, though your activities last night have already proven that. So, there's no need to panic about anything. However, I will emphasize the importance of restricting activities a bit. Nothing too stressful or acrobatic."

At her shocked expression, he laughed, a husky sound that reverberated in the small room. Unable to resist, Carla's laughter joined his. She couldn't sustain the mood she was in when he was deliberately trying to let her see how silly she was being.

"Okay, you win, Dr. Whitehall. I'm glad everything is fine. I *was* a bit worried, especially after what you said yesterday."

"Good, I'm glad you're fine. And call me Troy. Your son's going to be my godchild, so there is no need for formality between us. Gladys informed me that you're to come down for breakfast. I'm supposed to escort you down. Of course, I can't refuse Gladys's cooking."

"That seems to be the norm around here."

"Yes, we single men ache for a good meal every so often and, when your best friend's housekeeper is the best cook in Barbados, it's only reasonable to expect us to drop by every so often. So, if you're going to be here for a while, I'm sure we'll get to know each other."

"So, are you the final one or am I going to meet any other best friends dropping by?"

"It's only George and I you have to get accustomed to. Shayne doesn't keep many friends, but we've been best friends since high school. I'm the doctor, George is the lawyer and we three…"

"No special brotherhood name?"

"Nah, definitely not. We're way too egocentric to label ourselves with some common name."

"A bit arrogant, aren't we?" she said.

"Yes, it's my most redeeming quality." He laughed, a cheerful sound that didn't fail to encourage her to join him.

"And you're the doctor that I end up with?"

"Yes, you couldn't do any better, Ms. Nevins. I'm considered one of the best doctors on the island. And I'm in great demand. You should feel honored that you're under my care."

She glanced at him, noticing, not for the first time, the twinkle in his eyes. He was teasing her. She was not surprised, and found that she liked this best friend of Shayne.

"Can I be honest enough to say something?" he asked. His look of uncertainty was endearing.

"Yes, any man as confident as you shouldn't need to ask." This time she was the one teasing.

"Touché. I like you, Carla. Just don't hurt Shayne. If you do, we'll be the worst of enemies."

"So you're his protector, too. I'm sure Shayne doesn't need any protecting."

"Oh, I know he appears strong to everyone. But I've known Shayne since he was in his early teens. I've seen a side of him very few people have the opportunity to know. If you stay around, become his friend, you'll get to know him, too. Of course, I mean, beyond in the biblical sense of the word." He laughed. "You both seem to have taken care of that part of the relationship."

"Can we not talk about this situation as freely as you seem to want to talk about it? I'm not accustomed to talking with a complete stranger about my sex life."

"Complete stranger—I'm your doctor."

"That's only a temporary situation. After the baby's born, I'll be going back home."

"So, you *are* going back?"

"Yes, Shayne doesn't seem to have a problem with my leaving. In fact, he made it clear that he's not father material. Of course, noble individual he is, he made it quite clear that he'll provide for the child financially." Carla tried to keep the sarcasm from her voice.

"Shayne? That's what he said? I'm surprised. Though he's said for years he doesn't want any kids, I never really took him seriously," Troy said.

"I get the impression he's very serious. He's made it quite clear that my stay here is temporary. I'm sure that I'd be gone if you didn't insist that I needed to rest."

"I'm going to have to disagree with you. I know Shayne and, despite whatever he's said, he'll be there for that child."

And then he stopped and stared at her, until she looked away.

"You're in love with him." His words came at her simple and clear.

"Of course not."

When he smiled at her with that knowing look, she flinched.

"Of course not," she repeated firmly.

"It's not me you have to convince. You have to convince yourself."

With that, he smiled. "Gladys must be waiting for us. I'm enjoying the conversation, but my stomach is growling. I have to visit another patient, so I need to get my breakfast. Gladys promised me her special Denver omelette and I don't want to disappoint her."

"You may love this cooking, but I'm sure it will make me fat. I'll have swollen to twice as big as I used to be by the time I leave here."

"No need to worry, Carla. I'm sure Shayne will love you however you look," Troy said, before he raced out of the room, his laughter echoing down the corridor.

Carla stood, arms akimbo, before she followed behind him. She was convinced that all Bajan men were crazy.

Chapter 8

Several hours later, Troy had gone and Carla yawned. She was bored. With the restrictions imposed on her, she wasn't sure of how to occupy herself during the day. She'd enjoyed her breakfast with Troy. He was fun, and he kept her and Gladys in stitches with stories of his and Shayne's antics during their school days.

She'd been surprised by her disappointment when he'd finally left. She wondered how two people so totally different could be such good friends. Then she remembered that she and Sandra were as different as night and day, and they were the best of friends. She couldn't wait to meet George.

She'd finally finished her romance novel and loved it. She couldn't wait for her favorite author's next one. Meanwhile, she'd sit out here in the garden and enjoy the sunset.

She wished she'd brought her camera. She never went anywhere without one of several cameras she had purchased over the years, but when she'd left for Barbados, other things had been on her mind. In college, she'd been a bit of an amateur photographer. She'd even thought of being a professional photographer, but the expense involved in studying photography had deterred her from the field. Instead, she'd gone on to do the more practical business studies.

Fortunately, she enjoyed the energy and diversity of managing a chain of travel agencies and she loved traveling. Of course, carrying a camera with her every time she traveled allowed her to indulge her childhood fantasy, especially now that she could afford camera equipment.

She'd call Sandra and make arrangements to have her equipment sent to her so she could find something to do in the time she spent on the island. She also needed to make arrangements with the Immigration Department to extend her stay. She had no doubt that Shayne would take care of that and it made no sense trying to extend her visa on her own when he'd know what had to be done.

She reached for the phone and dialed Sandra's direct line at the office.

Sandra's perky voice came over the phone line after only two rings.

"Hello, thanks for calling The Traveler. This is Sandra speaking."

"Sandra, it's Carla."

"Carla, what's happened to you, girl? Here I am all worried about you and you haven't called. It's been almost a week since you left."

"Sorry, I meant to call. Unfortunately, I've been in bed for the past few days."

"In bed? With that Shayne Knight? You couldn't wait?"

"Sandra, I mean, literally in bed. I collapsed the day I arrived here and the doctor had to come see me."

"You collapsed? What's wrong? What did the doctor say? Is it serious? Girl, let me sit down. You got me feeling faint."

"I'm all right, Sandra," Carla reassured. "No need to be a drama queen. The doctor says I just need to get some rest and eat frequently."

"I knew it. I knew it. I keep telling you it's normal to eat three meals per day and on time. You have someone to take care of you?"

"Yes, I'm staying at Shayne's house. It's big and lovely. Shayne's housekeeper, Gladys, is a wonderful cook. She's definitely taking care of me."

"I still don't understand how you can eat so little. I just get a whiff of cheesecake and I gain three pounds."

Carla couldn't help but laugh.

"Are things good at the office? How's the new girl working out? I hope things aren't too hectic."

"So far, Jessica and I are managing fine and the new girl, Cindy, is a treasure. Teach her something and you don't have to show her again. You remember that girl we hired last year? I'll never get someone from the temp agency again. But don't worry about us. You take care of yourself and that baby."

"I will. I also need you to do me a favor. Can you send my camera equipment to me? Send it to the address I gave you before I left and address the package to Shayne Knight. Use our usual courier service since they ship to Barbados. I should get it in a day or two."

"Will do. I'll go by your apartment tonight since it's one of my nights to check to make sure everything is all right." She paused. "Can you hold a minute?" Carla heard her say. "Girl, I have to run. Someone just came in the store and Jessica has a client. I'll get that stuff out to you tomorrow. And please keep me informed about what's going on. Take care of my godchild."

For a while after the phone disconnected, Carla sat staring at it. She missed her friend and the warm camaraderie that existed between the two of them.

Here on the island she felt alone. She felt like an afterthought, but she needed to be here for her baby.

Shayne Knight scared her. Scared her because she knew her feelings for him went deeper than mere admiration. She remembered their lovemaking from the night before and her nipples tingled at the memory of his lips on her.

What was she going to do? There was nothing that she *could* do, but stay focused and try her hardest not to love him too much. She'd have her son and, as soon as humanly possible, she would fly back to Virginia and the real world.

She didn't want to be hurt, but she was prepared for the inevitable. On an island like Barbados, a person could easily be caught up in the fantasy that came with being in paradise. For the locals, the island's beauty and mystique were the norm. For the visitor, the island became a magical world of swaying palm trees, golden sands and shimmering waters.

Barbados was made for the night magic of romance. But when the night faded into day, the magic was gone and the reality of everyday life remained.

So her dream of romance was just that—a dream. She knew Shayne felt something for her, but were his feelings only connected to their two naked bodies and the heat of passion?

Carla wanted more than that. She knew that Shayne could be a good husband and father. Under the reserved indifference, she knew he could be gentle and loving.

Get a hold of yourself, Carla. The romance novels you read have created a monster.

Though she enjoyed the realism of the modern contemporary romance, Carla had always loved the world of the historic romance. She dreamed of the courtship of elegant ladies by knights in shining armor. Of course, her knight rarely wore his armor. In her dreams, he wore nothing.

She smiled. The irony of Shayne's last name played like a pun in her mind.

He was her knight.

Her elusive knight in shining armor.

Carla wondered where this would all end. What would become of her? Since her husband's death she'd had no desire to marry again or to have a relationship. Meeting Shayne Knight had changed all that. But she couldn't let him know that she wanted more.

All she could do was sit back and see how things turned out.

One thing she knew.

It wouldn't be easy waiting.

Later that night, when Shayne returned home, Gladys informed him that Carla had retired to her room. He was tempted to visit her, but changed his mind. What he really needed was a swim in the pool, something he hadn't done for several weeks. He'd eaten dinner with George and Troy, a monthly event he looked forward to, but he'd been distracted by thoughts of Carla and his son. He'd forced himself to relax and laugh out loud at George's dry humor. When he'd left, he was feeling much better, but Carla was still on his mind.

Of course, he had to endure ribbing from his best friends about his activities of the night before, something he still felt guilty about since Carla had fallen earlier in the evening. He should have been more considerate of her condition.

He also realized that Carla had somehow wrapped Troy and George in her magic circle. They'd both demanded that he allow her to make a good man out of him. Even George's initial skepticism seemed to have lessened, though he still had some reservations about Carla.

Shayne had smiled and laughed at their words, but now they lingered in his mind.

Under normal circumstances and, if he intended

to marry, Carla would be his ideal wife. Not only was she beautiful and sexy, she was an intelligent woman. She ran her own business and had a great education. Carla would make some man the perfect wife. The thought of her married to someone else didn't please him at all, and he wondered why. He knew it wasn't about his feelings for her, but he didn't like the idea of another man raising his child.

All this was getting too confusing for him. A few days ago, he'd been sure he didn't want too much to do with her or the baby. Now, he was reevaluating the situation and he was beginning to see things differently.

Shayne pulled his shirt over his head and slipped off his trousers. He stood in a pair of loose fitting boxer shorts. Since Gladys was the only one usually on the premises at nights and she retired early, Shayne felt free to swim in the nude.

Slipping from his boxers, he stood on the edge of the pool and expertly dove in. His entrance was smooth and clean, but the water shocked him with its chill.

He swam the length of the pool in record time, the slight discomfort slowly disappearing as his body adjusted to the cold.

When Shayne could do no more laps, he turned on his back, allowing his body to float on the surface. The cloudy night sky held very few stars.

He loved this time of night. On nights like these he'd lie in the pool and think of all the screwed-up things in his life—or about what was going great. He wasn't sure about his life at this moment.

Fortunately, he was slowly adjusting to the changes going on; he wasn't sure if he liked them very much, but he was adjusting. It was times like these when he really missed his brother and sister. He'd pretended to be so happy that they had moved on, but he couldn't stand the stillness of the house. At least Carla's presence helped.

When Russell and Tamara were home, there'd always been noise. Not the earsplitting noise that modern-day parents had to learn to endure. It was the warm vibrating sense of oneness with his siblings. He loved them more than life itself and working hard to give them the best he could had taken nothing from him. If he had to do it all over again, his brother and sister would still come first.

Unexpectedly, his mother and father came to mind. He remembered them clearly. Though his father had provided well, he knew the marriage had not been a perfect one. He remembered clearly the evenings when, after his father had picked him up from school, they'd go visit "Aunty Barbara." His father would never tell his mother about Barbara and Shane had promised his father to keep the secret.

To this day, he still saw Barbara on occasions in

the city. And he still blamed her for his parents'
death. That night, as his parents had left home to
go out to dinner, he'd heard them quarrelling at the
tops of their voices about her. His father had sped
down the driveway. An hour later, the police had
arrived at the house.

Shayne had vowed on that day that he would
never get married or have children. He didn't want
to be like his father and he didn't want to be caught
up in some supposed-to-be-happily-ever-after relationship, in which the two parties eventually realized that they no longer loved each other. Love,
as far as he was concerned, was not a long-term
commitment. It was simply racing hormones,
which cooled after a while, when one of the part-
ners was ready to move on to greener pastures.

But, yes, Carla did something to him. If the possibility of happily ever after was to become a reality
for him, it would have to be someone like her. But
their so-called relationship had no future since
its foundation was a weak one. A holiday romance
with someone who was practically a stranger was
definitely not a solid beginning for the possibility
of anything more permanent.

Shayne flipped over, determined to swim himself into exhaustion. Unless he did, he'd probably
end up in Carla's bed. He wanted her the way plants
needed water.

This intensity of feeling was not for him. His no-strings-attached approach to romance had seemed a good one, until he'd let his feelings get involved. And now he had to deal with the consequences.

He'd learned one thing from this situation. Never make love to a woman more than twice unless you plan to marry her. He'd made that mistake with Carla and now she'd worked herself into his system and he was no longer sure how to purge her.

But he was going to try. Even if it was only for a few hours.

For now, he would just stargaze, clear his mind of all that was going on in his life and dream of a future that was no longer complicated.

Carla's camera equipment arrived several days later and she almost screamed with relief. Boredom had begun to set in and the fact that Shayne seemed to be ignoring her didn't help her foul mood. In the morning when she awoke, he would already be gone and, when she retired at nights, he'd still be out.

She'd caught a glimpse of him one morning when she forced herself up and stood at the window to watch him leave. He wore his signature white shirt and blue jeans and the sight of him had stirred her in a profound way.

Today, however, she decided that she was going

outdoors to take a few pictures around the plantation. She'd been cooped up inside for too long and she ached to feel the warmth of the sun on her face.

She quickly took a shower, raced downstairs and gobbled down an excellent breakfast. She'd asked Gladys about the general layout of the plantation. Promising Gladys that she'd stay close to the main house, Carla set out to find a few scenic places to photograph.

Her first stop, a short distance from the house, was the small paddock where the horses were kept. When she arrived she saw two of the most beautiful mares. They turned immediately as she drew near, and she saw looks of caution on their faces. A young man, bent over a large bucket, straightened as she approached.

The stablehand was Todd. Gladys had told her about him.

He walked slowly toward her.

"You must be Ms. Nevins. Gladys told me you would be coming here to see de horses." Noticing the direction of her gaze, he added. "Dem beautiful, yes?"

"Yes, they are."

"Come, meet dem. Dem is sweethearts. Love when visitors come by."

He opened the small gate, allowing her entrance to the paddock.

Immediately, the horses trotted in their direction.

"See, they eager to meet ya. The black one is Thunder and the white one is Storm. Storm's the pregnant one."

"What lovely names!"

"Tamara named them. They both hers, but Shayne's the one who rides dem now Tamara not here. He also has his own horse, Mongoose."

"Oh, I wish I could ride," Carla said.

"Oh, you can learn. It's not difficult. Hold this, they love carrots."

He handed her the two carrots he held in his hand.

When the horses reached them, they both stretched to nuzzle him. However, they kept their eyes cautiously on Carla.

When she held the carrots out, Thunder turned her head as if to formally acknowledge her. When Todd touched her head, she moved toward Carla, reaching for the carrot before drawing it into her mouth.

The white mare, noticing the treats, reached for the carrot, which Carla had raised toward her.

Hands now empty, Carla reached out to touch Thunder, then Storm.

Finally, seemingly bored with the visitor, the horses trotted off before they started galloping around the paddock.

"Dem showing off," Todd said. "They like the attention."

Taking her camera bag from her shoulders, Carla quickly prepared to take the shots of the horses.

In the next thirty minutes she took a whole roll of film. She couldn't help it. The horses played, stood proudly at times and raced around the paddock at others.

However, she was able to capture one especially tender moment when they'd snuggled each other before lying on the ground, tired from their exercise.

Thanking Todd, Carla headed back to the house. She'd get some lunch and then take a short nap. She hoped she'd find something to do tonight besides watch television or read a book. The new James Bond movie was showing at the local cinema and she'd love to go see it, but when her host was never at home, it was impossible to go out at night.

She entered the house at the rear, finding Gladys at the sink.

"Lunch is ready," the smiling woman said as she turned toward Carla. "Did you have a great time?"

"Yes, I took so many pictures of the horses. Thunder and Storm are adorable."

"We had to promise Tamara we'd take good care of them. She spends hours outside with them. We weren't at all surprised when she said she wanted to be a vet. When she was young she used to fill the barn with stray animals from all around. I've helped to feed baby birds, abandoned kittens, even a baby monkey. However often we threatened to punish her, she would always find another stray. She would open her big sad eyes and allow water to pool. And poor Shayne, he couldn't resist her."

Carla laughed. "You must miss her."

"Oh, yeah. I miss her and Russell. Since they left, the house has been so quiet. They brought the house alive. I'd always know when they were at home. The house has a different feel. Alive with energy."

"I'm sorry I won't get to meet them."

"I'm sure you will. You're carrying their nephew, so I have no doubt you'll meet them."

At Carla's look, her smile softened. "Shayne told me about the baby. I hope you don't mind."

"No, of course not. I'd have been surprised if he hadn't told you," Carla said.

"He did say you have to rest, yourself."

"I'm making sure I do. I have a baby to take care of so I won't do anything silly."

"Good, and, since I'll be watching you and taking care of you, I'll make sure you don't over-exert yourself."

"Since I now have my cameras, the only thing I'll be doing is taking photos, reading and having the occasional swim."

"Sounds fine. However, right now, you need to eat something."

"Thanks, I am feeling a bit hungry."

Carla sat and Gladys placed before her a plate piled with salad, macaroni pie, corn on the cob and succulent ribs moistened by barbecue sauce.

Several minutes later, Carla burped, blushing with embarrassment when Gladys turned toward her and smiled.

"Good. Means you enjoyed the meal. I hope you like cornbread. I'm making some for dinner. Dinner will be relatively light tonight. Just fries and chicken with cornbread.

"Gladys, what are you trying to do to me? It takes me hours in the gym to keep to a size six."

"It won't matter much in the next few months whether you go to the gym or not. I can predict that you're going to gain a few pounds." And, as if proud of her wit, she started to laugh uncontrollably. Carla joined her, holding her stomach as tears poured down her cheeks.

"Man, I haven't laughed so hard and long in months."

"Good, at least I'm not the only one who needs a bit of laughter."

When Shayne entered the kitchen, that's how he found them, giggling like teenagers.

For a moment, he stood looking at them. At least, at Carla. She was so beautiful. He felt that now-familiar stirring in his groin. He hoped this wasn't going to continue for too long. He'd be constantly walking around aroused if this happened each time she came near him.

"I wonder what the two of you girls could be talking about that could have you giggling like schoolgirls. I hope you're not talking about me."

"Definitely not, Shayne. Not to burst your bubble, but there are a lot more interesting things for us girls to talk about than you. Isn't that so, Carla?"

Carla smiled, her eyes twinkling with mischief. "Or maybe we were talking about you. There are some stories I could tell Gladys about you that would curl her toes."

Shayne realized it was time to change the conversation.

"Carla, I need to talk to you about something important. Gladys, can I borrow her for a moment? I promise to send her back when we are through with our talk."

"That's fine. We'd finished our little girls' talk. You can have her all evening."

"That's fine. I just need a few minutes to discuss a personal matter."

"Okay, but I think it would be nice of you to take her out of the house. Take her on a drive and let her see some of the island." She paused. "Carla *needs* to get out the house," she continued.

"That's not necessary. I'm fine. I have a book I thought I would start this evening."

"Gladys is right. I'll go take a quick shower and I'll be back down. We'll go out. Have some fun."

She opened her month to say something, but Shayne beat her to it.

"I'll be down in ten minutes," he said. "I'll come get you when I'm done. And not another word out of you."

"If you insist. I'll wait down here for you, once I get my camera from the sitting room."

"Good, you'll have plenty of opportunities to take pictures. I hope you have enough film?"

She nodded. "Yes, I have enough."

"Good, I'm going up. I'll see you in a few minutes." With that, he turned and walked away.

When he came downstairs fifteen minutes later, Carla was waiting for him in the kitchen.

"Good, you're ready. Let's go. I'm going to look up some friends of mine and then we can stop at a tiny ice-cream parlor on the west coast."

"Now, how did you know that I loved ice cream?"

"Oh, my memory is fine."

She blushed, and he could tell that she remembered the night not too long ago when… Oh, the things they'd done with ice cream.

He hardened.

Again.

He was in for a long afternoon and evening. If only he could keep the image of a naked Carla from his mind…

They drove for a while without conversation. Not liking the tense silence between them, he said, "I'm just stopping here for a short while to look up two friends of mine and drop off some stuff for their mother."

"That's fine. I'm just trailing along for the adventure."

"No need to be sarcastic. If you really didn't want to come, you could have said so," he said.

"I would have accepted any invitation, but I really don't like to be coerced into doing things."

"My sincerest apologies. I really didn't mean to embarrass you. Let's call a truce and see if we can enjoy our evening. I really want your company."

Before she could answer, he turned the car into a short driveway and stopped in front of a tiny bungalow.

Two children raced from the house, coming to stop just in front of the car.

"Mr. Knight, you've come to look for us as you promised. Mom, said that you'd be too busy to come."

"I made a promise and I always keep my promises."

And then they saw her and their eyes turned in her direction.

The little girl was the first to speak.

"Is she your girlfriend, Mr. Knight? She's pretty."

"Yes, she is."

At Carla's sweltering glare, he grinned.

"Let me introduce her."

"Carla, this is Emma and Chris."

"Hello, Emma and Chris."

"Nice to meet you, Miss Carla."

"It's fine to just call me Carla."

The boy spoke. "I'm sorry, Miss Carla, but our mommy told us never to call adults by their first name, unless we know them well. She says it's disrespectful."

At the same time, a woman strolled from the house. She was slightly plump, but she was pretty.

"Mr. Knight, I'm sorry, Harry isn't at home."

"I didn't come to see Harry, Joanne. I just came to see the kids. I brought something for them. If that is all right with you."

"You've given them—us—so much over the past months. I can't let you keep giving."

"I know how much they like to read, so please allow me to bring them a few books whenever I can."

"Thank you. As long as it is just books. I'm glad they like to read." She turned to glance at Carla. "I'm Joanne."

"Sorry, I was about to introduce my friend, Carla. She's spending a few weeks with me."

"Mommy, she's Uncle Shayne's girlfriend. Isn't she pretty?"

"Yes, she is. Very pretty. Nice to meet you, Carla."

"You have two lovely kids. I'm just a friend of Shayne's, visiting the island. Of course, I must apologize for Shayne. He's misled the kids."

"Okay, I confess. But she's going to be my girlfriend, so I was only speaking about the future."

With that, he smiled and turned to the kids. "Come help me to get the books out of the car."

"Uncle Shayne, you have to read a story to us before you go."

"I wish I could, kids, but I promised Carla I would take her to someplace really special. She's not been feeling well and I want to give her a treat."

"To help her to get better?" Emma asked with a serious look on her small face. "You can rub her tummy if it hurts. Is she going to have a baby?" the child asked.

"Yes, and I'll do whatever it takes to make her better."

At Carla's glare he smiled. He was carrying this a bit too far, but Carla responded politely.

"Shayne, you must read to the kids. I'm sure getting where we're going could wait a few minutes."

For some reason, Carla was intrigued. She

wanted to see how Shayne would interact with these kids. She was already impressed with the comfortable rapport between him and them.

She wondered who they were, this family. She knew there was a husband, since Joanne had made reference to Harry and she wore a wedding ring. But what was their connection to Shayne?

"Carla, how'd you like to come in and have some iced tea while Shayne reads the story to the kids? They're going to curl up in the kids' playhouse and we can go in the sitting room and talk girl stuff, if you don't mind."

"Oh, I'd love a glass of something very cold. I love Barbados, but the heat of this season is a bit more that I can handle right now. My being pregnant hasn't helped, either."

"Then iced tea it is," Joanne said, as she led them into the house.

Carla turned to follow Joanne into the house, casting a glance back at Shayne and the kids. The picture she saw was not that of a man who claimed not to want kids, but of a man who found delight in being around them. Shayne's laughter made her dream of things that were not meant to be.

An hour later, Shayne, carrying Emma and followed by a yawning Chris, entered the sitting room.

"As you can see, Emma finally fell asleep after demanding I read most of the stories in this book."

"Good, it's about time she gets some rest. Both she and Chris were a bit restless this morning. Thanks for stopping by, Shayne, and for the books."

"You know, it's no problem, Joanne. Chris and Emma are wonderful. I like spending time with them."

"Feel free to drop by, anytime."

"I will. Well, we have to go. I've promised Carla some ice cream. You know what happens when a woman's pregnant. You have to give her whatever she wants to eat. So ice cream it is."

Again, Carla glared at him, and, again, he smiled.

She was going to deal with him as soon as they got in the car. Not that it mattered since he seemed to be in a jovial mood.

As soon as the car pulled off, Carla made her feelings known.

"How could you tell her that I'm your girl-friend?" she asked.

"Aren't you?" he replied.

"No, I'm not."

"So what do I call you? The mother of my child? My lover?"

At her appalled look, he smiled, and she felt like slapping it off his face.

"You arrogant son of a bitch," she snapped, her hands itching.

"Thanks for the compliment. I aim to please."

And then the strangest thing happened. Carla just found herself laughing. An unexpected fit of laughter.

"You're so crazy. I don't know what to do with you."

"Just do what you've been doing and I'll be happy and satisfied."

"Mr. Knight, you win. Just let's go and enjoy our ice cream. I'm going to demand three of the biggest scoops of my favorite flavors."

"As I said, Ms. Nevins, I aim to please."

"I could say that you're already doing a great job of pleasing me, but that would only boost your ego."

"No need to put your assessment of my prowess into words. Your body lets me know each time we make love and your eyes, they burn with fire. So, Carla, my dear, I'm quite aware of your response to me."

"I'm not sure what's happening to you tonight, but you're behaving like a randy schoolboy."

"Maybe, I *am* a randy schoolboy."

"Well, I'd prefer you to behave with a bit more decorum."

"Oh, I'll try to behave for the rest of the night, but to hell with decorum. I would never use that word to describe our relationship, in or out of bed. You're like me, you like it wild and hot."

Carla breathed in deeply. He'd succeeding in arousing her.

"I know you're feeling just like me right now, but I'll respect your wish. Tonight, we'll be just two good friends. We'll sit, have ice cream and talk about movies or music. But it won't change anything."

Carla knew that what he said was so true.

Chapter 9

The month of February came and went and the island's lush vegetation flourished with the gentle showers, which fell frequently. Valentine's Day passed without a raise of anyone's eyebrows and Carla had been glad for that. She passed the days reading. Gladys had taught her to knit, a skill that she'd never expected to enjoy. Of course, her first effort had been pathetic, and she joined Gladys in cheerful laughter when the baby booties she'd made looked far from anything she could recognize. Now, her skill brought "oohs" and "aahs" from her teacher.

Just over six months pregnant, she'd swollen to

almost twice her size and forced herself not to break into tears whenever she glanced at herself in the mirror, an action she found herself doing less frequently.

Today, however, Carla was bored. She didn't want to go look for the horses, she didn't want to read or watch television. She just wanted to get out of the house. If she stayed inside for another day she'd go crazy.

Shayne was most likely at one of the cane fields directing the harvest. She didn't know how he did it, but she continued to be amazed at his ability to keep going and going. From the middle of February, he'd disappeared, his focus on the harvesting of the sweet-smelling sugar cane.

When Carla woke up in the mornings, he'd already be gone and, at night, when he'd come in, she would already in bed. It was only on Sundays when he came downstairs dressed in shirt and tie that she saw him. He'd be off to church. Then, as was his habit, he'd spend the rest of Sunday with his old school buddies.

So Carla was bored. She needed to see another face besides Gladys. She needed companionship. She'd called Sandra on several occasions, but Virginia seemed too far away. She no longer felt a part of that world.

Barbados had worked itself under her skin and

she sometimes thought of living here. But she realized that moving to the island would not be a sensible move. She wasn't sure if she wanted to be in such close proximity to Shayne.

She'd love to go to the beach and take a walk along the sands. She wanted to take photos around the island and of the sun rising against a watery backdrop. She just wanted to feel less trapped.

Everyone thought she was fine, but she wasn't. She felt as if she was losing control of her life. At home, she controlled three agencies and loved the activity and pressure involved in making them successful. This leisurely pace failed to provide the stimulation she needed to totally enjoy her existence. Her only comfort came from knowing that her baby was doing fine and she was no longer losing weight. In fact, she loved the sense of fulfillment as she felt her body change with the growth of her child.

Carla was reaching for the remote with the intention of finding a show to watch when she heard the thud of footsteps coming down the hallway.

She turned slowly and awkwardly in the direction of the footsteps, surprised to see Shayne enter the room.

He wore a white polo shirt, blue jeans and pair of leather sandals.

"Morning, Carla."

Her breath caught in her throat and, for a moment, she could not respond to his polite greeting.

"No church this morning?" she asked, eventually.

"No, I've decided I need a day off. So how would you like to go to the beach? Go out to lunch? Gladys is spending the day with her sister who lives to the north of the island. She doesn't return until tomorrow so I thought it'd be a chance for us to eat out."

"I'd love to go out for lunch. It was kind of you to ask," she said excitedly.

"Good, there's a restaurant on the west coast that serves the greatest meals. George, Troy and I go there fairly often. Especially when Gladys is on holiday or when she goes to spend some time with her family."

"Of course, you could all learn to cook and you wouldn't have to eat out so often," she interjected.

"I assure you we can all cook. Maybe not as well as you or Gladys, but we can hold our own. One of these Sundays, I'm going to invite them over and we're going to cook up a storm."

"I look forward to it," she said, her response teasing. "Let's hope you are as good as you claim."

"I'm definitely good, but you'll have to see for yourself."

"I look forward to it. When do we leave?"

"About noon. I've made the reservation for one

o'clock. George and Troy will be joining us. They can't resist eating out. Hope you don't mind. Afterward, we'll go to the beach."

For a moment, she hesitated, unsure about spending time with his friends, but she did like Troy. "No, having your friends join us will be fine. When we go to the beach I'd prefer not to go in the water."

"Bring along a·book, and I'm sure you can still have some fun. George wants to meet you, and I'm sure Troy will be glad to see how you're doing."

"Can I go take some pictures of the Storm's foal? Gladys told me that she's adorable."

"I'll come with you. I was on my way to check on her, anyway. You go put on a pair of sensible shoes and then we can go."

"Okay, I'll go upstairs and be back in a minute."

"Take your time, Carla. I have a few phone calls to make first. I'll be ready in fifteen minutes."

With that Shayne turned and left her standing. there, but not before she caught a glimpse of how wonderful his butt looked in his close-fitting jeans.

A half hour later, Shayne watched Carla click photo after photo of the chestnut foal who stared at them with bold curiosity while its mother looked at them with wary eyes. The foal was a beauty. Already, her fragile legs had grown strong, allowing her to frolic around the corral. Now, she stood quietly, her clear black eyes, so like her mother's, staring at them.

His gaze moved to Carla. She appeared animated, the antics of the foal delighted her. He'd noticed that, though she tried to look happy, she often appeared sad. It had taken Gladys's prodding to make him see that Carla was bored and going nuts being stuck inside all day.

Yes, the harvest of the ripened sugar cane had started, but there was nothing to stop him from taking the odd day off to entertain her.

In reality, he'd been trying to avoid her. Being around Carla Nevins continued to disturb and confuse him. He always seemed to lose control of all his faculties when he was around her. He couldn't allow that to happen.

There was something about her that stirred him. He'd always heard people say that pregnancy made a woman radiant, and that was definitely the case with Carla.

Last night, when he'd arrived home, an irate Gladys had finally blown her fuse and given him a piece of her mind. She'd expressed her disappointment at his neglect of Carla and she made a statement that had slammed him right in the face and left him troubled for the whole night.

Gladys had been right. He'd been fighting his

feelings for Carla from the day he'd found her standing in his sitting room.

From that moment, he'd wanted to protect her, but most importantly, he'd wanted to love her. He wasn't sure if he was *in* love with her, but she made him feel things that scared him.

Carla made him gentle.

At that point, Shayne heard her squeal. The foal had walked toward her and placed its nose in her outstretched hand. Carla's face lit up, totally filled with joy.

Shayne swallowed rapidly, an uncomfortable lump in his throat.

"Carla," he shouted, "we have to go. It's getting late."

"I'm sorry," she said. Her face had lost its joy.

"We'll come back another time. I'm sure the foal won't mind," he teased.

At his words, she smiled and her face softened again.

In silence, they walked back to the house, each lost in troubled thoughts.

When they arrived at the restaurant, George and Troy were already there. Shayne led her to the table where they sat drinking glasses of frothy local beer.

When Shayne introduced her, George stood and shook her hand. Like Troy and Shayne, he was handsome, but he was short in comparison to his two friends. While Troy and Shayne stood over six feet, George was just over five feet. Next to his friends, he was short, but he made up for this with an impressively muscular body, and he knew it. His caramel complexion also contrasted with the deep-mahogany skin tones of Shayne and Troy.

"Shayne, you dawg! You didn't tell me how beautiful she is. And, Troy, I'm disappointed. I thought we told each other everything. Carla, it's nice to meet you. I've heard so much about you. Well, except the fact that you're beautiful." With a dramatic flourish of his hands, he pulled out her chair for her to sit.

"Thank you, George," Carla replied, sitting. "It's always nice to meet a gentleman. I'll have to say we're equal. I've heard a lot about you, too, but Shayne definitely didn't tell me how handsome you are."

"Okay, okay, let's not start a mutual admiration society. We're here to eat and I'm so hungry I could eat a cow," Troy said, his stomach growling at the same time to emphasize his hunger. "I was in surgery all night and early this morning,"

"I'll call the waitress," George said. "She promised to come as soon as you arrived."

As if on cue, the waitress appeared, handed them

menus and told them she'd be back in five minutes to take their order.

When she returned, Shayne gave their order. They'd all agreed on the special of the day, a grilled strip-loin steak studded with cracked peppercorns and served with rice, potatoes and vegetables.

While they waited, George asked Carla question after question about almost every aspect of her life, and, though she responded politely to each query, she was relieved when the waitress returned with their meals.

For a while, they ate in silence and Carla savored the meal while watching the three men eat with relish.

She was convinced that one of the things the trio had in common was their love of good food. She wondered where they put it all because none of them had a spare inch of fat on his body. At least, as far as she could tell on Troy and George. She did know for sure that Shayne was all lean muscle.

For the rest of the meal, Carla watched them joke and laugh, their love for each other obviously deep and genuine. Their camaraderie reminded her of her own relationship with Sandra. She missed her friend and needed a woman to talk to and share all that she was dealing with. A long-distance call didn't help much. She wanted to see Sandra. Maybe she should give her a call tonight and invite her for a weekend.

And then an unexpected thought flashed in her mind. She wondered if Sandra would find George attractive. Oh, she'd have to count Troy out since Sandra didn't care too much for doctors. She'd taken them off her list of men to date.

She laughed, only realizing she done so out loud when three pairs of eyes locked on her.

George broke the silence. "I'm hoping that joke wasn't on me."

"To be honest, I was thinking how I'd like my best friend to meet both of you."

"Both of us? I'm sure Troy won't be interested. He doesn't have the time for women right now. It's all about becoming the world's greatest doctor."

"Thanks for speaking on my behalf, George, but he's right Carla, I'm focusing on my practice. No time for the fairer sex."

"See? So when do I get to meet your friend?" George asked.

"I'll talk to her tonight, but I'm hoping that Shayne won't mind her coming for a short visit."

Carla turned to Shayne, but, before he could respond, the waitress came to their table to find out if anyone wanted dessert. Of course, the men ordered the largest pieces of cherry cheesecake she could find. When she was gone, Shayne turned to her.

"Of course, your friend can come to visit. Just let me know when she's coming so I can get a room ready for her and can arrange for her to be picked up at the airport."

Suddenly, Carla felt elated. Sandra could come. She couldn't wait until later to call. For a few days, she'd have someone to talk to.

Maybe she could come for the upcoming weekend or the following one?

Not that it mattered, she just wanted her friend here.

A few minutes later, they were on their way to the beach, completely satisfied with the meal. George was singing an off-key version of one of the most popular calypso songs on the airwaves.

Carla sat on a beach chair, shaded by the large umbrella Shayne had rented for her. For a while, she sat reading, but became distracted by the antics of the three friends in the water.

After spending an afternoon with the three men, she was convinced they were crazy.

What she did find interesting was that Bajan men didn't wear the tight-fitting swim trunks their counterparts in the States wore. The islanders preferred to wear normal boxer or basketball shorts. Shayne and Troy wore loose-fitting shorts that did little to hide their lean, toned bodies.

Carla tried to keep her eyes off Shayne, but she found her gaze glued to his slightly hairy chest and the ribbed six-pack stomach. She'd seen him naked on several occasions, but there was no one sexier than he was at the moment.

Of course, George preferred to go with the tight-fitting swim trunks, which he claimed emphasized his assets. He took every opportunity to showcase his physique to the large number of women on the beach.

But Carla realized something about George. He was more talk than action. He pretended to be a "playa," but he was far from being one. When he wasn't on show, Carla realized that he was a lot like Shayne. George was troubled and insecure about love and relationships and, behind his insecurity and loud bravado, he was really a sensitive, caring individual. She liked him and hoped to see more of him.

Troy was also like Shayne, quiet and introspective. He was not unaware that he was attractive, but didn't flaunt it as George did. She'd seen him in both a professional and a social setting and she liked what she saw. Despite his serious nature, he was fun to be around.

Carla found their relationship an unexpected one, but she realized when the three of them were together they brought out the best in each other.

She heard loud laughter and realized they'd come out of the water and had joined a group of men playing football on the sand, all except George who was coming in her direction.

"Mind if I sit here with you?" When she nodded, he sat on the sand next to her chair. "I'm really not the sporting type and would prefer to sit and chat with a beautiful woman," he said.

"George, since we are more likely going to see a lot of each other and could probably become friends, it may be better if we get something out of the way."

"And what is that, may I ask?" he said, his tone humorous.

"I can see beyond your macho persona, so let's just be real with each other. I don't want to spend the time—when I could be getting to know Shayne's best friend—getting to know his alter ego."

"So, we're not wasting time." His tone had gone from flirtatious to serious. "Shayne is one of the only friends I care about, so let me just say that you're going to have to deal with me if you hurt him."

"I don't see how I can possibly hurt Shayne when he wants nothing to do with me or my child. You're his lawyer, I'm sure you're aware of the arrangement he intends to put in place. And, I assure you, I'm not after his money. I have plenty of my own."

"So why are you here?"

"Exactly what Shayne told you. I just wanted to make sure my child knows who his father is. I want nothing else, as you well know."

"Good, I'm glad to hear that. So, we're cool with each other. I want to like you, but I'm putting things on reserve. Hope you don't have a problem with that?"

"Definitely not. You're protecting your best friend. That says a lot about who you are. I think I'm going to like you, but I'll hold *that* on reserve. Listen, Shayne and Troy are calling you. You need to get back and have some fun. I have a book I want to finish, and I'd prefer to read without your sexy butt next to me," she said with a wary smile on her face.

"So you think my butt is sexy?"

He kissed her on the cheek quickly and ran off yelling to his friends at the top of his voice.

Carla smiled at his antics. He was incorrigible, but she liked him. He was lots of fun, but she'd seen a serious side of him, too.

She flipped the pages of her book, quickly finding where she'd stopped before George'd disturbed her.

Soon, absorbed in her romance novel, she didn't feel the eyes that continued to stare at her.

That night when she called Sandra, her friend agreed to come for a weekend when she could get a flight. The next morning, she called to say she'd arrive Friday night.

On Friday night, just after nine, Carla sat on the patio waiting for her friend to arrive. Sipping a chilled glass of Gladys's special lemonade, she thought of all she had to tell her best friend.

When a pair of headlights appeared, coming up the driveway, Carla tried to contain herself.

Before the car could come to a total stop, the door on the passenger's side flew open and Sandra jumped out.

"Carla, Carla, I'm here." Sandra raced up the steps and hugged her. "Girlfriend, you look good. Pregnancy suits you. You look lovely, girl!"

Carla couldn't help but laugh. Sandra was always the drama queen.

"Shayne, thanks for picking Sandra up at the airport."

"No, problem, it was a pleasure. I'll take her luggage to the guest room next to yours."

"Sandra, let's go inside and get something to eat. After that long flight I know you must be hungry."

"Girl, you know the routine. What they give you to eat on the flight ain't worth shouting about. Five minutes after eating I was hungry again, but there was this really cute guy sitting next to me, so I spent the whole flight flirting with him. Had to tell him I'm visiting my boyfriend when he offered his number. When he told me he was a doctor, that turned me off immediately."

"I have no idea what your problem is with doctors, but Shayne has a friend who's a doctor and he is so fine. And you must meet George. He's a riot."

"Sorry, girlfriend, but I'm not interested in meeting any men this weekend. Maybe if I came back sometime before or after the baby is born. I'm definitely not in a man mood this weekend. This is your weekend."

"Great, because I'm looking forward to having some fun."

By now, they'd reached the kitchen. Gladys was there sitting at the counter, watching one of her late-night shows and sipping her nightly glass of wine.

"Gladys, this is my best friend, Sandra. I told her all about you," Carla said brightly.

Gladys stood, pulling Sandra into a healthy hug. "It's nice to meet you. I'll get a plate out for you. You must be hungry."

"It's nice to meet you, too. I *am* hungry. I have heard a lot about your cooking, so I can't wait," Sandra replied.

"So Carla has been talking about me?" Gladys asked.

"Yes, but only good things," Sandra assured the older woman.

"I would hope so," Gladys said, and laughed, as she filled a plate with mashed potatoes and gravy. When she was done, she placed the plate on the table. "Carla," she said, "do you want anything to eat?"

"No, Gladys, I'm still full."

"Thank you, Carla. And Sandra enjoy your dinner. I'm going to retire for the night. I have to go into the city in the morning."

"Nice to meet you, Gladys," Sandra replied. "I'm sure I'll see you tomorrow. Thanks for preparing this wonderful dinner for me."

"The pleasure is mine. You have a good night. Carla, just leave the things in the sink. I'll wash them in the morning."

When Gladys was gone, Sandra quickly gobbled the meal down. "Carla, I see what you mean. Gladys *can* cook. I'll hire her and pay her twice as much as Shayne does."

"Sorry, but she's too much a part of this family to leave."

"Oh, well, can't say I didn't try," Sandra said.

"Ready to go up to your room?"

"Yes, I'm tuckered out, but we can chat until we're sleepy. Just like we do all the time. I have lots of questions for you."

"I'm sure you do," Carla said, and led the way to the guest room.

* * *

"So, how's the baby doing? You're looking well. And I see you've put some weight on that skinny frame of yours. I told you that you were working too many hours and not eating enough."

"No need to complain, anymore. I'm getting all the rest I need now. But I'm going crazy with boredom. I'm so glad you came to spend the weekend."

"I'm happy to see you, too. I say we spend this weekend relaxing and pampering ourselves. This is going to be our special girls' weekend. My flight's on Sunday evening so we only have two days to catch up on all the gossip. Girl, I have so much news for you."

"I'm supposed to be taking it easy, but there's a pool and I have to show you the new foal. She's just a few days old."

"Carla, I really don't want to talk about no foal right now. Tell me about Shayne."

"What about Shayne?"

"I want to know everything. Are the two of you still rumbling between the sheets?"

Carla didn't answer, the heat warming her face.

"Girl, are you and that hunk still doing the dirty? Can't blame you. If I lived under a roof with a man as fine as he is, I'd be jumping his bones every night," Sandra said.

"I'm sure you would be. But I'm not even sure

why I'm here. Shayne has no intention of being the kind of father I want for my son."

"Carla, you need to give him some time. Not every man is prepared for an unexpected pregnancy."

"Maybe you're right. I think I came here expecting too much. I don't want anything much from him. I just want a father for my son. I know what it's like growing up with a mother and no father. My foster mother treated me well, but I always wished I had a father."

"He seems like a good man. I'm sure, when the baby is born and looks just like him, he'll melt. I think he's just scared."

"Scared? Shayne Knight? One of his friends said the same thing. Maybe what you say is true. We'll just see what happens," Carla said softly.

"Well, girlfriend, the jet lag is about to kick in and I need to get my beauty sleep."

"Me, too. The little one has been doing somersaults all evening," Carla said.

"Well, you can stay right here and keep me company. Go change into your nightgown and we'll chat until we fall asleep. I've got to tell you about Jessica and the office. You'll never believe what I caught her doing with…"

"Okay, okay, don't say a word. I'll go to my room and get into my nightwear and I'll be back in five."

Carla rushed out of the room.

She couldn't wait to catch up on all that had been going on at the office.

The weekend passed more quickly than Carla would have liked. It seemed as if, in no time, she was kissing her best friend goodbye. As she watched her friend enter the gate to board her flight, a wave of sadness washed over her. She wished Sandra wasn't going, but she knew that her friend had to get back to the business.

As she sat in the car driving back to Shayne's home, she thought of the wonderful time they'd had together. She missed Sandra so much, but the short time with her would make it easier to handle the days to come.

"Did you and Sandra have a good time?" Shayne asked.

"Yes. Thanks for allowing her to come and stay."

"I'm glad she came. She's a lot of fun, and it was good to see you laughing," he said.

"So I don't laugh?"

He nodded. "I don't see you laugh too often."

"I don't see you laugh too often, either," she observed.

"Well, that's true, maybe we're two of a kind. And I do laugh when there's something to laugh about."

"Maybe I need to do something to make you

laugh more often. My coming must have taken all the joy out of your life."

"Don't be silly, Carla. I assure you, I've come to grips with what's happening to you and what's happening to us. I've decided, however, to deal with each day as it comes. Your being here is far from being an imposition."

"So why are you avoiding me."

"Am I?"

"You are."

"Okay, I admit it. I have feelings for you and, to be honest, I'm not sure what's going on."

"So, instead of dealing with your feelings, you've decided to run from them. You've been avoiding me," she said.

"Maybe I ran, but at the time, I thought it was the best thing to do. I'm sorry if I hurt you, it was not my intention."

"I understand. I feel the same way. I'm not sure how I feel, so maybe, as you say, we need to accept that something is happening and deal with it one day at a time. I don't want you to worry about anything. We have to think about the baby," Carla said.

"I agree. Your health and the baby's are my priorities. Everything else is secondary. But let's not talk about this now. Your friend has just left and you want to think of the good time you had with her. Tell me a bit about the business you manage. I want to get to know you better."

For the rest of the drive, Carla told Shayne about the travel agency her late foster mother had owned. She told him how her foster mother had left it to her when she'd passed away. Carla explained how she'd built the business and had expanded it to three agencies in five years. She now had a staff of more than twenty workers.

Shayne asked question after question and only when the car pulled into the plantation's driveway did he stop.

Stepping out of the car, her spirit felt light.

"I'm going to go check on the foal. You go on up to bed."

"Thanks for taking me to the airport and letting Sandra come to visit. I really appreciate it." She turned to walk toward the house.

"Carla," he whispered her name.

She stopped.

He came up behind her, placed his arms around her and turned her to face him.

When she turned, they stared at each other, their actions and thoughts suspended in time. And then he lowered his head, kissing her gently on the lips. It was the briefest of kisses, the whisper of the wind.

"Have a good night, Ms. Nevins," Shayne said.

And, with that, he turned and walked in the direction of the stables.

Chapter 10

During the night, Carla woke up in excruciating pain. She lay for a while, wondering what could have caused it. She hoped it wasn't the baby.

A few minutes later, another flash of pain hit her, causing her to scream and forcing her to sit up.

She slipped from the bed and tried to stand, but the sharp pains in her stomach were too intense.

Carla sat on the edge of the bed wondering what to do. She tried to stand again, but her legs were weak and she lowered herself to the bed again.

Was it the baby?

Please, God, don't let anything happen to my baby.

She was scared.

Where was Shayne? Had anyone heard her scream?

Oh, God, help me!

The door flew open and, immediately, the room was brilliant with light, causing her to close her eyes to escape the brightness.

Slowly, she opened her eyes. Shayne stood before her, his eyes frantic with worry.

He touched her shoulder. "Carla, what's wrong?"

"It's the baby. Something is wrong. It's too early, Shayne. I'm scared."

"Stay calm. I'll call Troy," he said, moving to grab the cordless phone on the bureau next to the bed.

He spoke to the person on the other end and slammed the phone down.

"Troy says I should get you to the hospital as soon as possible. He'll meet us there. Do you think these are contractions?"

"I'm not sure, but the pain woke me up and then I had another one just before you came. I'm having some spotting, too."

"Come, let's get to the hospital. Where's your robe?" He asked, "I need to put something over your sleepwear. I'll get Gladys to bring you more clothes and things later. I don't want to waste time."

"Shayne, I can spare time to put a dress on. We just need to be calm," she said softly.

Seeing her look, he turned his back and walked toward the window. A few minutes later, she said, "It's okay, I'm ready."

He turned, catching a glimpse of the concern on her face. She wasn't as calm as she was trying to pretend, and he felt a surge of pride at how she was handling the situation.

He moved toward her, taking the small bag she carried in one hand and taking her hand with the other.

"Fortunately, I parked the car in the front and left it there. Let's go."

They walked slowly down the stairs. Gladys was waiting at the bottom.

"Gladys, you can pack a small suitcase of things Carla will need if she has to stay in."

There were tears in Gladys's eyes.

"Take care, Carla. The baby will be fine."

"Thanks, Gladys."

"Come, Carla, we must go. I'll see you in a while, Gladys."

Within minutes, they were heading to the Queen Elizabeth Hospital. On the way, Carla had another contraction. Shayne tried as much as he could to reassure her that everything would be fine.

They reached the hospital in record time and,

when they pulled up at the emergency entrance, Troy was already waiting there for them.

"Shayne, I'll take care of everything. You go park the car and then come inside."

Troy helped Carla out of the car and Shayne moved off quickly, reluctant to leave her for too long.

Since it was early morning, finding a parking spot took little time and, soon, he was back in the emergency room.

When he entered, he glanced around the crowded room. No Troy.

He sat in one of the empty seats. A few seconds later, he stood, feeling foolish when he realized there was no reason to be standing. He sat again. Where the hell was Troy?

Minutes later, Troy appeared through a swinging door.

Shayne jumped up.

"Is she all right?" he asked.

When Troy hesitated, his heart almost sank.

"She's definitely in labor. We're trying to stop the labor, but I've sent her up to the delivery room, just in case."

"Troy, she's only six months along. What about the baby?"

"I'm going to make sure that baby's given the best care, Shayne. I'm Carla's doctor and I've had a few premature patients. You have my word, I'll take care of them both."

"Thanks, Troy. I'm glad you're the one who's taking care of her."

"I have to head to the delivery room now, because I don't want to leave her on her own for too long. I'll get one of the nurses to give you directions to the room. I'll keep you posted.

Shayne watched as he walked away, fear gripping him in a way he didn't think possible.

Shayne closed his eyes. His eyelids felt so heavy.

Gladys sat in the chair next to him, her eyes closed, her breathing even. She'd dozed off again. She needed the rest.

"I'm sure Troy will soon be out. Everything will be okay." George broke the silence.

Shayne wished everyone would stop saying that, but he held his words. These were his friends. They knew he was worried.

"I know. It's just crazy not knowing what's going on. I should have gone into the delivery room with her," Shayne said.

"And you'd have probably passed out. You know how you are with blood. Troy has to give his full attention to Carla and the baby. He wouldn't have time to pick you up off the ground."

"I just feel that I should be doing more." He wished his hands would stop trembling.

"I'm sure that in the next few months you're going to have to be waking up in the middle of the night to nurse baby Shayne. You should get your rest now," George said, trying to lighten his friend's mood.

At Shayne's look of horror, George laughed. "Shayne, I didn't literally mean you." He paused at Shayne's sigh of relief. "You haven't done this baby thing much, have you?"

"I'm going…"

Shayne jumped up as he saw Troy walking briskly in their direction.

George stood and the noise woke Gladys.

"Okay, you can all relax. Carla is doing fine. She was a bit groggy, but she's fallen asleep. She'll be in her room in a few minutes, but, for now, Shayne is the only one who can see her."

"The baby?" Gladys asked.

"He's doing fine under the circumstance. Of course, for the first few hours, he'll be monitored closely. He's a fighter. Come on, Dad, let's go see your new little family."

Shayne smiled sheepishly at them and then turned to follow Troy.

They walked in silence for a while.

"I'll take you to see the baby, first. Carla's sleeping. Let me prepare you. He's very small. Under four pounds, but his heart is strong and all his organs are working."

"And Carla?"

"She did good, Shayne. She's a trooper."

Turning right at the end of the corridor, Shayne followed when Troy entered an open elevator. It moved quickly, stopping at the next floor.

"We're here. We'll go into the room and I'll give you a gown to wear. You won't be able to touch him. He's in an incubator that controls his body heat."

In the room, Shayne donned a green hospital gown and followed Troy through a room at the end of the hall to another room completely made of glass.

"Which one?" Shayne whispered.

"The one just below us. With all the hair on his head."

Shayne looked at his son and a powerful fear gripped him. His son was so very small.

"Damn, he's so tiny, Troy."

"Yes, Shayne, but I haven't lost a preemie yet, and I have no intention of losing him. He's my godson."

"This is crazy, but I love him already, Troy. I just looked at him and felt a fear so strong, I know that he's mine and I have to protect him. I can't let him die."

He didn't realize that he was crying until, he felt the tears run down his cheek, but he didn't care. This helpless tiny bundle was his son.

He felt Troy's arms go around him.

"Shayne, my brother, you know he's in good hands. I'll leave you here and go check on Carla. I'll let you know when she's awake. The nurse will take care of you until I get back."

"Thanks, Troy, for everything," Shayne said.

"Shayne, it's nothing. We're family, aren't we?"

"Yes, we sure are. Would you let George and Gladys know all is well. And, if you would, please ask George to take Gladys home. I'll call them in the morning."

When Troy left, Shayne continued to look at his little boy. Although his son was all scrunched up and almost purple all over, Shayne still thought he was the most beautiful baby he'd ever seen. And he was proud of him. Despite coming into the world a bit too early, Shayne could see he was a fighter. *Come on, little one. You're a Knight.*

Tubes and gadgets Shayne knew nothing about buried his son beneath their sterility, but, to him, they were instruments of hope. His son was a fighter, but Shayne knew he couldn't do it alone.

Shayne felt an overwhelming urge to talk to him.

So he did.

Shayne told his son about his uncle and aunt, and about Gladys and George and Troy. He even told him about the new foal that had just been born.

And Shayne told him about his mother.

He felt proud of Carla, too. How she'd handled all of this. Having to deal with a pregnancy and making the decision to involve him in his son's life.

Under all the chaos around him, Shayne thought he saw the baby smile.

He knew that he needed to do one more thing before he left to see Carla. Closing his eyes, he thanked God for giving his son life. He knew the working power of God's grace. He was, by no means, the best of persons, but he had an overwhelming respect for his maker. Time and again, God had seen him through the toughest times, and he knew this would be one of those times.

When he opened his eyes, Troy stood there.

Shayne smiled.

"Carla is awake and asking to see you," Troy said. "She wants to see the baby, but I had to convince her that she needed to rest for a few hours."

"I'll go talk to her. Let her know our son's doing fine."

He followed Troy out of the room and down another long corridor before Troy stopped in front of a door.

"You can go right in. I've asked them to place a small cot in there so you can get some sleep. I knew you'd want to stay here tonight."

"Thanks, Troy. I know I wouldn't be so fortunate if you weren't here."

He turned to his friend, placing his arms around him and hugged him, hoping that he could embrace the strength he knew his friend possessed. He'd definitely acquired a deep admiration and respect for what Troy did.

His only hope was that his friend could save his son.

Carla shifted her body, groaning at the slight soreness in her lower body. Where was Shayne? She wanted him here with her. She wanted to hear about her son. Troy had told her he was a fighter and the prognosis looked good, but he would be monitored closely for at least the first twenty-four hours.

The door to her room pushed open and Shayne entered. She felt like crying.

Before Shayne could speak, she asked, "How's he? Is he okay?"

"Yes, he's doing as well as can be expected. He'll pull through. He's a fighter...and he looks a lot like me."

"I want to see him, Shayne." Her voice was filled with anguish.

"I know you do, but you need to take things easy right now. I promise I'll take you to see him as soon as Troy allows you to leave the room. I'll stay here to make sure our son gets all he needs. Troy will give him the best care."

"I'm going to see him tomorrow, no matter what," Carla said.

"I'll make sure you see him. But, right now, you need to get some rest. I'll sleep for a bit and then go back to see how our boy's doing."

"We're going to have to stop calling him our boy and our child. Maybe if we give him a name it'll help to make him more real." •

"Have you thought of a name?"

"Yes, I wanted to name him Darius."

"I like that name. It's strong. I'm sorry to say that his middle names are going to be George and Troy. Years ago, while at school, we promised that our first sons would have each other's names as middle names. So our son is Darius George Troy Nevins Knight," Shayne said.

"Nevins Knight?" she asked.

"Yes, it's only fair. I want him to carry my name and I'm sure you want him to carry yours," he replied.

"That seems reasonable, though I wouldn't have a problem with just Knight. It's a strong noble name and I'm not sure if I want him carrying Darius

George Troy Nevins Knight around for the rest of his life," she said, grinning.

Shayne joined her in laughter. "I'm in total agreement. So Knight it is. See, that wasn't too difficult." He paused when she yawned. "Now it's time for you to get some rest."

"I am feeling a bit tired."

"Good, I'll turn the light off. If you need me, just wake me up. I'm right here."

When the light went off, Carla closed her eyes, willing the sleep she knew her body needed to overtake her, but the events of the day played like a movie in her head: The early labor and the way Shayne had taken charge of the whole situation. Today, he'd lived up to his name. The proverbial knight in shining armor. Not in the typical sense of the word. But he'd shown her a side of him that was brave, noble and gentle.

Somehow, he'd put all of his reservations about fatherhood behind him and done what he had to do. She'd been a bit surprised when he'd claimed the child as his own, knowing his initial feelings about his part in their son's life.

Maybe seeing their child pulled on his paternal instincts. The Shayne she saw now was one who had definitely accepted his son.

She sighed, feeling the trembling of her hands. She was afraid. She wasn't scared to admit it. She was in love with her son's father and she seemed to no longer be in control of her feelings. It made no sense to try to fight her response to Shayne. Their initial meeting had been a coming together of two willing bodies, but getting to know him as a person was slowly making her see things differently. So much had changed in a little over two months.

Where had all her ideas about marriage and commitment and children gone? Where was their initial no-strings-attached arrangement?

It no longer existed for her or Shayne. She knew his feelings had changed. Instead of the wary looks and occasional flashes of desire she had seen in his eyes, she now saw something different.

He looked at her with a gentleness that spoke of his growing emotion. Maybe he wanted something more.

She knew she wanted something more.

Well, she needed to get some sleep. She wanted to be strong in the morning. She wanted to see Darius. She needed to see her son.

She closed her eyes only to find God in the silence. With tears in her eyes she thanked Him for letting her son see life.

When she finally fell asleep, a beautiful smile touched her lips.

* * *

During the night, Shayne woke up to the sound of the door opening. He jumped, the light from the corridor almost blinding him, but he realized it was Troy.

He slipped from the cot, putting his sandals on and headed for the door. Outside, he closed the door behind him and stood waiting to hear what Troy had to say.

"Shayne, don't worry. He's all right. I just came to see if Carla was asleep or if she was in pain."

"She's fine. We talked about the baby. I'm going to see Darius now if the nurse will let me."

"Darius?"

"Yes, we decided on a name. Our son is now Darius George Troy Knight."

"You remembered. It's a bit of a mouthful, but it sounds strong, especially the Troy part," the doctor said, with a broad grin. "The nurse will let you see him now. I need to go home and get a few hours sleep. I have to work the morning shift at the office but one of my friends will cover for me here until midday. I'll be back then. Want me to bring some stuff for you?"

"Gladys is coming tomorrow. You can call her and let her know you can pick her up. She doesn't like to drive much, these days. Says the traffic is too heavy and her driving that antique manual shift car that she has doesn't help."

"Antique? That's a genuine 1972 Volkswagon."

"Okay, I know your obsession with cars. However, I have a son to go visit. Have you heard from George yet?" Shayne asked.

"Yes, he called earlier. He said he'd be here sometime in the morning, after he meets with a client. Sends his congrats and reminded me about the name thing."

Shayne laughed. "How is it that both of you remembered something that we promised each other years ago?"

"You remembered, didn't you?"

"Touché. Let's go see Darius. I'm sure he's looking for his dad."

Gladys placed the phone in the handset and sat on the stool at the counter. She didn't feel like being in the kitchen, but she'd promised Patrick she'd bake a cake for his wife's birthday. Maybe the activity would keep her mind off of the events of the past twenty-four hours.

Just after ten o'clock the night before, she'd been chatting with Shayne when they'd heard a noise from upstairs.

Carla!

Shayne had immediately leapt to his feet and raced upstairs. She'd followed quickly behind.

When she'd realized it was the baby she'd rushed back downstairs to start the car, so that all Shayne would have to do was get in and drive.

She had only experienced fear like this once before—when Shayne's mother and father had died in the accident—but a dark fear had gripped her in the waiting room. Carla was only six months pregnant, and Gladys knew the fragile nature of a preemie.

She'd wanted to stay at the hospital, but knew that someone had to be at the house. Shayne had promised to call her with any developments. She'd grown to love Carla and she knew the confident, independent woman was the best thing that had ever happened to Shayne.

Oh, things were going slower than she'd expected but she realized that Carla was just as stubborn as Shayne was. Even so, it was inevitable that the two of them would realize they loved each other.

She knew that the next few months would be a trial for all of them. Having a premature baby fell short of the wonderful experience of having a healthy newborn. She knew the reality of it. Years ago, her sister had given birth to a little girl born at just twenty-five weeks. After they'd watched the tiny bundle fight for four weeks, the baby had passed away.

Gladys remembered how exhausted her sister had been during the weeks caring for the child, and she'd experienced a severe depression when the girl died. It had taken them months to recover.

She hoped Shayne's son was a fighter, just like his dad. If he was as stubborn as his father and mother, he was well on his way to living for years.

Gladys closed her eyes and hoped that her prayer would reach heaven before it was too late.

Chapter 11

The next morning, Shayne woke up to the sound of rumbling in the room.

The nurse had given him a chair to sit on in the nursery for the remainder of the night. He'd decided to stay with Darius instead of going back to Carla's room. His neck hurt because he'd spent most of the night sitting on the uncomfortable chair before he'd drifted off to sleep.

He rose, immediately heading to the area where his son slept. Again, he felt that prick of anxiety and fear as he saw the tubes connected to his son's body. He breathed in deeply, emitting the air slowly when he realized his son's chest still moved up and down.

His son was still fighting.

It was only when he felt the wetness of tears that he realized he was crying again. He didn't care. The helpless bundle of life was his blood. He closed his eyes, finding it difficult to control his emotions at this time, so he allowed his thoughts to drift upward. God would understand how he felt. For the second time in hours, Shayne gave thanks to Him for giving his son life.

And he asked forgiveness for his unwillingness to accept the responsibility that was his. He felt a deep shame at the fact that he'd wanted so little to do with his son.

Seeing his son had made a difference. In the back of his mind, however, he'd had visions of a healthy bouncing baby and now he was the father of a son who needed him. Each time he glanced at Darius he felt a love so overwhelming that he hadn't known it was possible. He loved his brother and sister so deeply that sometimes it hurt, but this feeling was different. Russell and Tamara could take care of themselves, but his son needed his strength and determination.

I'm going to take care of you and your mother, Shayne thought, but he did not speak the words. He knew that, somehow, his son could hear him.

Son, you keep fighting. You were born to live.

He touched the glass separating him from his son, hoping that Darius would feel his touch.

Boy, you have a big name. You're probably going to think we're crazy when you get older, but you're Darius George Troy Knight.

He turned, reluctant to leave his son behind, but he wanted to check on Carla. He was sure she'd been trying to convince someone she wanted to see her son.

He thanked the nurse for allowing him to stay during the night and left the unit. Despite his tiredness, he walked quickly down the corridor, coming to a halt outside Carla's room when he heard voices. He knocked.

"Come in." It was Troy.

When he walked in, Troy stood by the window and Carla sat in the chair next to the bed.

"Shayne, Carla has been sitting here waiting until you arrived. She wants to see her son, so I've given her permission to go. However, you must make sure she takes it easy. The nurse will give her all the information she needs, the same things she told you last night," Troy concluded.

"I'll take her, but I have to leave the hospital for a while so I expect you to watch over her for me. I have a few things I have to take care of this morning, but I'll be back by midday," Shayne said to his friend.

"Good, that sounds fine. I have some rounds I have to make before I head to the delivery room. I have a few patients who've been admitted. I'll walk you to the nursery. It's close to my office," Troy said, turning to leave the room.

Shayne helped Carla to her feet and led her from the room. He fell in step with her, keeping his pace at a reasonable enough rate for her.

Reaching the nursery, Troy informed Carla he'd be back to see her later and that a neonatal specialist would come see her later that afternoon.

With Troy gone, Shayne followed Carla into the unit, watching her face to make sure she was all right. He waited patiently for the nurse to give Carla her gown and explain the do's and don'ts of the unit. Her induction completed, he helped Carla slip on her gown and then he put his own on. Shayne watched for any signs of discomfort and, though Carla appeared calm, he noticed the clenching of her hands on her gown. She was as nervous as he had been last night when he'd seen his son for the first time.

He guided her in the direction of the room where the incubators were.

For a while, she stood quietly, watching her son with unblinking eyes, until Shayne realized that tears were trickling down her cheeks.

She turned and walked briskly from the area, stopping by the nurse. Shayne didn't follow. She needed time to come to grips with what her son looked like.

He noticed that Carla held something in her hand, and then she headed in his direction again.

"I wanted to make sure I wiped my face before I touched him. I don't want to cause any problems with my tears." She turned toward her son.

"He's so tiny, but he's beautiful." Her voice was filled with emotion.

"Yes, he is, isn't he? He looks just like his dad," he teased.

"For sure, he does."

"Troy says he'll be on the ventilator for a while. He only weighs three and a half pounds so he has a long way to go. He did say that his Apgar scores were not too bad for a preemie. The doctors will do all they can, but we also need to put him in God's hands."

"I've already talked to Him. I'm trusting that He'll give our son a long life." He heard the hope in her voice.

"Carla, let's just have faith. The fact that he's still alive means that God has plans for him."

"I hope He does. My faith is not as strong as yours. I know what it is like to suffer a loss such as this would be, so if I seem a bit skeptical, it comes from personal experience."

With that, she turned toward Darius. She opened

the incubator as the nurse had instructed and touched him for the first time.

For a while, she continued to touch him gently. When she took Shayne's hands unexpectedly and guided them to the child, he felt a sense of dread. His hands were too large and heavy and he didn't want to hurt his son in any way.

"Just be gentle," Carla whispered. "You won't hurt him."

When his hands connected with his son for the first time, he closed his eyes, enjoying the softness of his son's skin.

Does Darius realize that we are here?

If what the nurse had told him was true, his son knew he was there and was already bonding with his parents. It was one of those things that had no logical explanation, but, as she said, there was a spiritual link between the parent and the child.

When the nurse came to inform them it was time to go, they were both reluctant to move, but knew they had to conform to hospital policy.

Outside, Carla stopped suddenly, tears coming down her cheeks. Shayne placed his arms around her and she buried herself in the comfort of his arms.

All the while, Shayne could only tell her, "Everything is going to work out. He'll be fine."

But there was something special about holding her in his arms. He knew that he wanted her there for the rest of his life.

Two days later, Carla was released from the hospital, but she didn't want to leave. She wanted to stay at the hospital to make sure that her son was being treated well. Only a promise from Troy that he'd stop by and look in on Darius often convinced her to leave. Even though the unit would only allow her to visit with her baby from nine o'clock in the morning until seven o'clock in the evening, being under the same roof as her son for those hours would make sleeping at night much easier.

Carla knew that she was being paranoid, since the hospital was probably the safest place her son could be, but she was his mother and she wanted to be there with him.

That night, as she sat in the passenger's side of the car, she could think of nothing to say to Shayne. In fact, he was as quiet as she was.

"I miss him, too," he said, "but Troy promised us he'd take care of him. I trust Troy with my life."

"I know that I'm being silly. I've seen Troy with him and know he loves him. Darius couldn't want a more devoted godfather or a better doctor."

"Yes, we're going to have to make sure that his godfathers don't spoil him."

Carla laughed. "That's true. Did you see all the toys those two brought to the hospital? I'm not sure where we're going to put all of them."

"No worry. I've already hired a company to take care of converting the room next to yours into a nursery. Fortunately, the room is between our rooms so I'll make sure there are connecting doors between his room and each of our rooms. When he leaves the hospital, I know you'll want him in your room until he's strong enough to sleep in his own room."

"Shayne, I don't want him to d—"

"Carla, don't you dare say it. Our son is not going to die. How can you think like that?"

"I'm just being realistic. I don't want to get too attached to him and then lose—"

"We're not going to lose him," Shayne interjected, his voice laced with anger. "We're not going to lose him," he repeated.

Carla did not respond.

For what seemed like hours they rode in silence. She could feel the anger boiling inside her. Not at Shayne, but at herself. She was scared. She was so scared that she might lose another child.

"I'm sorry, Shayne," she finally said. "I didn't mean to be pessimistic. I need to tell you something so you'll understand."

"What is it?" She could still hear the simmering anger in his voice.

"Almost three years ago, I lost my husband."

"You were married?"

"Yes, for almost five years. He died in a car accident. I was seven months pregnant and I lost the baby. I vowed that I never wanted to get married again. I didn't want another child.

When I came to Barbados, I came with the intention of just enjoying myself. I wanted to start to live again. And you gave me the chance to do that. I felt alive for the first time in years. I was finally ready to move on with my life."

"I know exactly how you felt. I felt the same thing. My parents had passed away and I'd spend the past ten years taking care of my brother and sister. I didn't date, didn't hang out with anyone besides George and Troy. I wanted to do something different, something daring and exciting. You provided that for me."

"You mean, our affair in paradise? We both got more than we bargained for," she said.

"Yes, we sure did. But the result of our actions has given me something that I never expected. I love my son. From that first night when I saw him, I knew that I loved him and would do anything to save his life. We need to talk about this a bit more later, when this is all over and we're thinking clearly. I know I want my son in my life."

She looked at him, shocked at his words, but she saw the genuine pain in his eyes.

"Okay, we'll talk about this when he's home and we're not giving in to the emotion of the moment," Carla said.

"Now I'm going to turn on the radio and we're going to relax and enjoy the rest of the drive home. No talking about the past," he said. "And, positively, no more crying."

"I'm in total agreement. I just want one thing, when we get home, we have to call the hospital and then, if you want, we can watch a movie."

"That's fine with me. I think we both need a bit of fantasy escape right now."

When the car turned into the driveway, they were greeted by a sea of bright lights. Gladys must have turned all the lights on since she knew they were coming home.

When the car pulled up, Gladys raced out of the house, followed by George and Troy.

As soon as Carla stepped out of the car she felt the older woman's arms around her, and she felt the slight prick of tears.

"So how's my boy doing?"

"When we left him, he was fine," Shayne told her. "Of course, we have the devoted attention of godfather number one to thank for his comfort and care."

"I thought I was godfather number one," George whined. "How did Troy get the top spot?"

"Oh, you're both number ones. My son has two godfathers who're both crazy, so it's only fair that you both hold that coveted position. Does that meet with your satisfaction?"

"Yes," the two devoted godfathers said in unison.

"Good, since that's settled, can one of you help Carla into the house, while I get our things out of the car? And, Gladys, it's okay to release Carla now. I'm sure she's hungry and wants to have some of whatever delicious meal you've created."

"I'm going to have to bow to the experts," she said, releasing Carla from her grip. "The two gentlemen you see before you are the ones who made the meal, so I'll escort Carla into the house and let them do the final preparations. My only contribution to the meal is setting the table, something I had to do when I realized that neither of them totally understands table etiquette. I am now aware of the reason why neither of them is married."

With that, she took Carla's hand and led her into the house leaving Shayne and his two best friends standing with their mouths wide-open.

George burped loudly, rubbed his protruding tummy and stretched his hands in the air.

"That meal was delicious. I couldn't eat another thing."

"I should hope not," Shayne said. "After your second serving I stopped counting. And, by the way, a cook should never indulge in self praise as an indication that the meal he created was excellent. Though, I must say, the pizza isn't half bad," he teased.

"If we were not in the company of two delightful and beautiful young ladies, I would respond to your observations with language not fitting for the fairer sex."

"I didn't even realize there was something that stopped you from speaking your mind," Troy said, joining the friendly ribbing, which was a part of the close relationship they had.

Carla had observed them during the meal and despite her attempt not to, had burst into laughter at the anecdotes each of the men shared about each other. Of course, the stories had become so farfetched she wasn't sure which were true and which were not.

She yawned. She was a bit more tired than she realized. It was really time she went up to bed.

As if seeing that as a cue for their departure, Troy rose, only to be pulled back down by Shayne.

"Damn, Shayne, I was about to make a polite exit after I'd bid your lovely guest farewell. I have to be at the hospital in a few hours. Of course, most of the pizza must be gone before George leaves."

At that point, George pulled himself from his seat, groaning and complaining about having eaten too much.

"As Troy has said, it's about time we left this wonderful party of five and headed off to our humble domains. Of course, since all of the pizza has not been eaten, I'll wrap a slice or two in foil so I can have it for breakfast."

Shayne and George's roar of laughter startled her. "Make breakfast, George? After all these years we know that you still don't have a stove."

"In this modern technological world, there is no need for such a primitive appliance as a stove. Don't you realize that they have been replaced by the more modern microwave and the countertop grill? See what happens when you have a woman to do all the cooking for you? You never learn to use a simple invention like the microwave."

"I think it's about time for the two of you to leave, but I want to talk to you about something important before you go. If Carla's yawn is any indication, I'd say she's ready for bed and, of course, Gladys is trying to cover her own yawns with her hands."

"Well, since you've noticed, Shayne, it might be a good time for me to take my leave," Gladys said. "Come, Carla, we're off to bed. The menfolk can clean up and have their little man talk. We ladies need to get our beauty sleep."

"Good night, boys. I'm sorry I have to retire so early, but I've been through an exhausting experience, so I need my rest. Thanks for dropping by. We must do it again if Shayne is willing to put up with your raucous behavior." Carla stepped forward and placed a kiss on each of their cheeks. "Troy, please take care of my son."

"I will," Troy replied.

"So, don't I get one, too?" Shayne asked.

"Sorry, Shayne, goodbye kisses are reserved for the guests. Gladys is waiting for me." With that, she turned and followed the yawning Gladys out of the room.

When they had disappeared, Troy and George turned to Shayne.

"I wanted to ask both of you the same question so I thought it would make sense to ask you now that both of you are here."

"So what's the earth-moving question?"

"I want you to be my son's godfathers."

"That's the damn earth-shaking question you want to ask us?" George shouted.

"Can you keep your voice down? Yes, I wanted to do it right."

"Shayne, it never ever crossed my mind that I wouldn't be your son's godfather." Troy chuckled. "Your question is bit of a redundancy. Of course, I know you couldn't be too sure about George, so asking him about taking on responsibility makes a lot of sense to me."

"Boy, you're lucky you're my best friend and I don't swear. I'd give you a taste of my favorite Bajan four-letter word."

Both Shayne and Troy burst out laughing.

"George, you ain't got no shame. You does cuss like a pirate," Troy said in his best dialect.

"Okay, but only when I get angry."

"Yeah, sure. All I can say is that the woman you marry is going to have to keep soap in every room of the house. She's going to have to tame you and make you into a different person."

"Man, be fair. Am I that bad? I'm going to have to take a good look at this. Especially now that I have a godson. I don't want him picking up any of my dirty habits."

"George, man, don't fret yourself. You need to clean it up a bit, but we love you still, always did, always will. You're like the brother I don't have," Troy said, putting his arms around George's shoulders.

"And you know I feel the same way. We go back a long way," Shayne said, adding his arms, until they formed a circle.

"Man, we haven't done this for a long time."

"Yes, maybe things are about to change."

"Change? What you talking 'bout?"

"Shayne and Carla and the baby. That's change."

"You're going to be next, Troy," George added.

"Oh, so you're goin' to be the last to go?" Troy asked.

"Definitely. I'm the big Bajan playa."

"Yeah, it's going to take a strong woman to snare your heart, but, when you fall, you're going to have it bad," Shayne said.

"Like you got it now?" George snickered.

There was silence.

"Yes, like I got it now," he eventually said.

"Oh, hell, Shayne is in love!"

Chapter 12

Time passed slowly during the next few weeks, with both Carla and Shayne settling into the comfortable routine of going to the hospital each day. Some days, Shayne would drop her at the hospital, go off to a meeting or take care of some business matter, but he'd always arrive at the hospital a few hours before it closed to spend some time with his son.

One morning, in the fourth week of Darius's stay, Carla arrived at the hospital to discover that her baby was missing from his incubator. Immediately, she panicked, but the nurse on duty gave her the good news. The nurse had been informed by the doctor that she should put the Knight baby in a regular crib.

Carla almost screamed for joy and, when she held her son in her arms for the first time without any tubes attached to him, she cried soft tears.

Later in the afternoon, as she sat holding her Darius, her eyes focused on his face, she looked up and saw Shayne entering the room.

The look on his face spoke volumes, and she noticed the glistening of moisture in his eyes.

That night, as they drove home, they were both silent and contemplative, but there was a sense of lightness, as if a physical burden had literally been lifted off their shoulders.

For the first time in weeks, Carla felt relaxed, as if she wasn't running on adrenaline. They exchanged pleasantries instead of the usual talk about Darius and his progress. That topic seemed unnecessary. But, as on every other night, Carla felt the presence of the man who sat next to her.

This evening, however, she recognized an awareness of him that she knew had been there, hovering at the surface. Because of her focus on Darius, she'd placed all thoughts of the last time they'd made love in a secret place.

Her body tingled with anticipation and she found herself glancing at Shayne. His focus remained on the road ahead, but she realized from the way he held himself that he, too, was aware of the subtle heat between them.

When the car pulled into the driveway of the plantation, she could feel the heat burning inside her and knew he could feel it, too.

When the car came to a stop, she opened the door, stepped out and moved toward the entrance, then stopped to wait for Shayne.

Together, they walked to his room.

When Shayne closed the door behind them, he pulled her into his arms, holding her as if nothing else in the world mattered. He turned her around, unzipped her dress and allowed it to fall to the floor. He slipped quickly from his shirt and trousers and soon stood naked before her.

Shayne led Carla to the bed, allowing her to lie first before he joined her. He wanted her, and knew that she wanted him, but he wanted this to be different. He moved toward her, placing his body against hers and drawing her even closer, his arms around her.

His erection strained against her, but he wanted to hold her. Later, they would make love, but he wanted to love her now.

Shayne placed a hand between them, finding the centre of her womanhood. His fingers touched the sensitive nub and he rubbed it gently, enjoying the way she twisted and wriggled with the building pleasure. He slipped a finger inside her, wanting to give her more pleasure. Her legs tightened around his hand and he knew she wanted release.

When her body tensed, he placed his lips on hers and captured her cry, drawing her closer as she trembled and shuddered with the intensity of her orgasm.

When her breathing stilled, Shayne drew her near.

He kissed her forehead gently. He'd never done anything so selfless in his life. He'd wanted to make love to her, but if he'd done it, it would have only been for his gratification. He'd wanted to give her all the pleasure.

So many things were trapped in his mind that he wanted to express, but he wasn't ready yet. He'd changed, his feelings for her had changed and he knew, clearly, that he wanted this woman and wanted to spend his life with her. He wanted to have other babies with her, wanted to wake up next to her in the morning. He knew he'd never get tired of her.

This time, he wanted to do things right. He wanted to be sure what he felt was love, but he knew he'd never felt this way about any woman before.

Shayne glanced down at Carla. She'd fallen asleep. She appeared peaceful and content.

He slipped from the bed. He needed a shower. He moved quietly, not wanting to wake Carla.

In the shower, he turned the water on, loving the feel of its coolness against his body. Carla's scent lingered and he closed his eyes, his need for her as strong as it had been the first time he'd laid his eyes on her. As expected, his penis grew erect and the temptation to pleasure himself was overwhelming.

And then the door eased open and the shower curtain moved aside and Carla stood there.

"We wouldn't want to waste that, would we?" she said, her voice heavy with desire.

She stepped into the shower, her gaze focused on his erect penis. She moved toward him, placing her body firmly against his. She moved slowly against him, the movement stimulating his penis until he felt he would burst.

When she gripped him with her hand, he felt a bolt of heat race along his erection causing him to tremble. Her hand on him was warm and stroked him firmly, until he could take no more and he felt that sudden rush of pleasure. His knees buckled and he almost fell to the ground.

He breathed deeply trying to bring his body under control.

Carla reached for the shower gel. Rubbing it into her palms, she spread it on his body, lingering to caress his already throbbing manhood, though he used all his willpower not to lose control.

Shayne shivered.

He loved her touch. He closed his eyes as her hands continued to work their magic.

When she was done, he returned the favor, soaping her body gently, until her breasts peaked and he wanted to touch her all over. He placed a nipple in his mouth and she screamed with pleasure.

He wanted to make love to her again. Wrapping a towel around her, he led her from the shower to the bedroom where he placed her gently on the bed.

Shayne raised himself above her, knowing he could wait no longer. At the same time, he captured her lips in a kiss. He entered her slowly, until he felt her grip each lengthy inch of him.

And then he began to stroke her with a firm steady rhythm and with every stroke Shayne felt as if he'd come home. Carla moved in time with him. Pausing in midstroke, he gripped her legs, wrapping them around him.

And then he stroked her again, moving his body in a slow circular motion that allowed him to touch each corner of her womanhood.

When Carla indicated she wanted him to lie on his back, he complied, his excitement heightened at her request for control.

On his back, he watched as Carla raised herself, then lowered her body slowly onto him. Shayne gritted his teeth, his eyes focused on her. And then she proceeded to ride him, an experience that almost blew his mind. In the past, he'd always been in control, but, this time, he felt vulnerable. He felt as if he were giving himself to her, body and soul, as if they were equal participants in this intimate dance of selflessness.

For a while, he watched her, enjoying seeing her wild and uninhibited. She moved up and down on him, a slow steady grind that caused his toes to curl and his body to ache for release.

Instinctively, he started to move, thrusting upward with each of her downward movements until he felt himself deep inside her.

And then he felt a flash of lightning and white heat scorched his body. He felt the muscles in his stomach contract and his penis stiffened one last time. The muscles of her vagina gripped him and, when he cried, it was the cry of a man who had taken a leap off a cliff and found himself soaring.

His whole body exploded, and the intensity of his release drew a cry from him that echoed in the room. He felt Carla collapse on him as her body shook uncontrollably.

Shayne closed his eyes, loving the feel of Carla's body on his and he wrapped his arms around her and drew her closer.

And he continued to hold her until he drifted to that magical place where knights and ladies fall in love.

In the middle of the night, Shayne woke up to find Carla sitting on the window seat, looking out into the night, the silvery, pale moonlight caressing her. Shayne experienced an emotion so powerful that he squeezed his eyes shut and opened them again to make sure she was real and he was not dreaming.

She was still there.

Shayne slipped from his bed and walked toward her. Carla turned at his approach and reached out for him. When he reached her, he hugged and kissed her, enjoying the feel of her lips on his.

"How do you feel?" he asked, his hands touching her.

"I'm okay," she replied. "A bit tired, but good tired. I'm not sure I could do that again tonight."

"Me, either," Shayne said.

They laughed.

"So where do we go from here, Carla?"

"I don't know. But I know things have changed."

"Yes, things have changed. Having a child makes a world of difference to how you view life. I'm not sure it's only about Darius. My feelings started to change long before he was born."

"You want to get married?" he asked. He knew he was abrupt, but that was what he wanted.

"Married. I'm not sure if I'm ready for that," she replied. Her words were honest, but they still hurt. "I care about you, Shayne, but I'm still not sure I want to make that final commitment yet. I want to get to know you, first. And I don't mean all of what's been going on. I really want to get to know you."

"So you want me to court you?" he asked, placing his hands on her back. She was soft, her body still warm.

"If that's what it takes. Maybe we should take things easy. I know that we're attracted to each other, but we need to find out if we care about each other enough to take this a step further."

"Okay, I'll agree with you, for now."

"So maybe we should cut out the lovemaking and see if there is more to what we feel?"

"No sex? I'm not sure if that's a good idea." He could tell his hands were working their magic. She was breathing heavily.

"Well, I think it's a good one. I want to know that this relationship is about more than a roll in the hay. I want to see if we can be friends." She reached for his hands, pushing them away.

"But we're friends. You have my word on it. You're my best friend."

"I thought that position was reserved for George and Troy?"

"It was, but you're my best *female* friend."

"Okay, then answer a question. Do you know when my birthday is? Do you know which college I went to? You didn't even know I had been married."

At his silence, Carla smirked. "See what I mean? We don't know each other. And I won't get married to someone I don't know."

"So how do you propose we get to know each other?"

"Well, we could do the usual thing."

"Which is?" he said dryly, sarcasm evident in his tone.

"Okay, I'm done." Carla attempted to stand. "You're not taking this seriously, so I won't even think about us being friends. Maybe, I'll just do as I planned originally. When *my* son is old enough, I'll go back to Virginia."

"Over my dead body," he said vehemently.

"Oh, so this is the man who wanted nothing to do with his child. Just the occasional visit. Now you want to be father of the year." When she said this, the expression on Shayne's face changed and she realized she'd gone a bit too far, but before she could apologize, he replied.

"You're right. I'm being unreasonable and

maybe I'm thinking with another part of my body. I know how I feel about you. I could make love to your every night and never get enough of you, but as you said, we don't know each other. So, yes, we need to rectify that."

"I didn't mean to be hurtful… I'm sorry. I want my child to grow up knowing both of his parents, but I'm not sure if two parents not knowing each other is a good thing."

"I can see I have no choice but to agree. I might have done things differently, but since this is the way you want it, I concur."

"I admire your sense of honor. Of course, since the focus of this current experiment is to discover if we can be friends as well as…"

"*Lovers* is the word you're looking for, I'm sure."

"Yes, lovers, there will be no intimate contact for the next few weeks. Of course, you are an honorable man, so I'll expect you to refrain from any attempts to seduce me."

"As you wish, my lady. I'll be the noblest, most gentle knight you've ever read about in one of those romance novels you and my sister seem to be addicted to. Of course, knights always had tricks up their sleeves…or should I say under their armor." He stood and bowed gracefully.

Carla smiled.

"Since I must be honorable, it is time I take my

leave." At her look of disappointment, he smiled and continued. "Of course, the easiest way to resist temptation is to avoid it and since I'm addicted to making love to you, it would only be the beginning of breaking my word to you if I remain. So, my fair lady, I wish you a pleasant night."

With that, Shayne turned and left the room.

A shocked and disappointed Carla looked longingly at the door thinking, *He'll be back.*

An hour later, when she fell asleep the house was still. No telltale footsteps heralded his coming.

She would be sleeping alone again, but this time she was in Shayne's bed.

The next morning, Carla woke to the sound of knocking at the door. She dragged herself out of the fog of weariness and sleep-deprivation and crawled from the bed.

When the knocking persisted, she shouted, "Coming," but the sound coming from her throat was a pathetic crackle.

She flung the door open and there stood Gladys.

"Good morning, Carla. Shayne asked me to give you this message. He has to go into the fields today, but promised he'd be at the hospital, as usual, this afternoon. I'm to drive you there."

"Thanks, Gladys. I'm going to come right down as soon as I take a shower. What time is it?"

"It's just after nine."

"I'll be down soon. I'd like to get to the nursery as soon as possible. Darius knows when I'm there and he expects me to be there early."

"I was coming up to wake you this morning, but Shayne told me to let you sleep a bit later. Said you didn't sleep much last night." Of course, Gladys said this with that silly smile on her face. Carla was glad she'd made the decision to end the sexual component of her relationship with Shayne for a while. At least, she wouldn't have to endure the knowing glances from Gladys, anymore.

"I'll go get ready now. I'll just take some cereal. I need to start taking care of my weight."

Gladys's response was a loud snort.

"Weight? Since you had that baby of yours, you've lost all the baby fat around your waist. You don't need to lose any more by eating only bird helpings. You need good, hearty meals to take care of that little one you have in the hospital. I've done some scrambled eggs and biscuits."

"I'll be down," Carla said, closing the door as Gladys walked away, muttering about young women who wanted to starve themselves to death.

Carla smiled at the ongoing battle between her and Gladys. Of course, Gladys was winning, but the twenty minutes of exercise she did each morning was helping to restore her figure to her former size six.

Showering quickly and choosing a simple pale-blue dress, Carla dabbed on a touch of her favorite perfume and slipped into a comfortable pair of slippers.

Downstairs, with Gladys breathing down her neck, she ate her eggs and the fluffiest biscuits she'd ever tasted and hastened Gladys to get to the hospital.

Carla held her son and watched as he looked at her as if she were the best mother ever. Recently, he'd taken to smiling, his eyes sparkling with life.

She thanked God daily for the gift He'd given her and, though Darius was tiny, she'd noticed with pride the way he was filling out. At first, she'd been scared to hold him. He'd looked so fragile and helpless; she'd been literally frantic, since she was sure she'd drop him. But she never did. She'd absorbed the information the nurses and doctors had given her eagerly. She knew that the only way she could care for her child was if she knew the best way to care for him.

She had no doubt that Shayne would help. He'd been equally interested in knowing all he could about her—their—son's care.

She watched him hold his son with pride for the brief moments allowed and she would see his mouth moving as if he were talking. Every time she saw them together, she cried.

"So, how's my boy doing today?" she whispered to her son. "You're doing fine. Well, that's good. I'm assuming it's time to have your feed?"

She sat, holding Darius as carefully as possible and slipped her breast from her bra. She remembered when she'd first breast-fed him, she'd felt that sharp sting when his mouth had gripped her and started to draw his nourishment.

Carla had experienced a sense of oneness with him as he'd suckled. A strange feeling had built inside her until she'd realized that motherhood was not only a physical, biological process but an emotional experience in which mother and child bonded in a profoundly spiritual way.

She glanced down at Darius. His eyes were focused on her as he drank. She knew part of Shayne's pride came from the fact that his son carried those startling midnight-black Knight eyes. In years to come, Carla knew her son would be a heartbreaker.

Just like his dad.

She wanted his dad, but she'd made the rules.

No sex.

When he'd asked her to marry him last night she'd wanted to scream yes at the top of her voice, but she didn't want things to happen that way. She wanted a husband, friend and father to her child.

The sex had been good, in fact, it was always incredible, but, as she'd said last night, she wanted more. She wanted to know the man whose child she'd borne. She wanted to know him in the most intimate and emotional way possible.

And that wasn't possible if, each time they came in contact, they ended up in bed together. Not that she didn't want to pounce on him each time he came near. Her body had ached last night while she'd waited to see if he'd come back to her in his room.

His resolve had been clear. He'd agreed to what she wanted, but he was going to make sure she suffered in the process.

She'd wanted to give in last night. She'd risen from the bed several times to go find him, but good judgment had literally forced her back into the lonely, empty bed. She'd tossed and turned all night long, only falling into a restless sleep in the early hours of the morning.

She wondered, for the hundredth time, where this would all end. She wondered if she were unwise to dream of a happily-every-after ending like those in the books she loved to read. Some of her friends had told her that endings like those were just a fantasy, and not a part of the real world.

Maybe they were right, but maybe, just maybe, some people were able to find happiness and love.

That's what she wanted for herself.

Darius gurgled playfully, and she smiled, lowering her head to kiss him on his cheek.

She cradled him, starting to sing softly.

Who would believe that motherhood was so amazing and that, in just six short months, she'd go from being a busy businesswoman to being a mother!

She laughed, remembering her meeting with Shayne in October the previous year.

She'd demanded that there be no strings attached and here she was, attached to the Knight family in a deeply emotional way.

She lowered her head again, kissing her son on his forehead.

When she placed him in his cot, she stood next to him, touching him and watching him smile at the angels.

When Shayne walked into the room and realized his son was gone, he panicked, but the nurse quickly pointed toward where Carla sat, holding Darius.

He walked over to them.

"Shayne, Darius is out of intensive care."

"So, he's really doing well?" he asked.

"Yes, they say we'll be able to take him home in a few weeks, a few days before his original due date. He's over four and a half pounds, that's more than a pound over his birth weight."

Shayne didn't know whether he should shout or jump for joy. The way he was feeling, he wanted to do both.

He glanced down at his son, the boy's black eyes staring back at him. When Darius smiled, Shayne knew that everything was going to be just fine.

At eight that night, Carla stood before the mirror in her room, ready for her date with Shayne. She wasn't even sure how to define it, but he'd told her clearly it was a date.

Instead of arguing, she'd allowed him to call it whatever he wanted to.

Shayne was in for a big surprise.

The image looking back at her pleased her. Not much of the weight she'd put on during her pregnancy remained.

The black dress hugged her figure, emphasized her slender hips and the firmness of her breasts as well as her long legs.

Retrieving her handbag from the bed, she stepped from the room.

She paused at the top of the stairs, when she realized that Shayne waited for her at the bottom.

Shayne was handsome in a rugged kind of way, but seeing him in formal dress only served to transform him into a sophisticated man of the hour. He wore a black blazer, gray slacks and a pale-lavender shirt, which emphasized his dark-chocolate complexion.

"You look beautiful. No one would ever think you'd just had a baby."

"It wasn't easy, but thanks to the pool and some aerobics, I'm having some success."

"Oh, the pool. Gladys did tell me that you try to go every morning before you leave for the hospital. But, come, the dinner we're attending begins in an hour."

When she reached the bottom of the stairs, he placed his hand on her elbow and led her toward the front door. The perfect gentleman, he escorted her to the passenger's side of the car, made sure she was comfortable and then took his seat.

They drove in silence for a while before she asked, "What's the function we're attending?"

"It's just a small dinner party that I've been invited to by a friend who runs one of the other plantations on the island. She throws a great party."

She? Carla wondered about the mystery woman.

"No need to get jealous," Shayne said.

"Jealous? I'm now even more convinced that you're crazy. What should I be jealous about?"

"If you say so. I'm sure you don't have a jealous bone in your body."

"I don't."

Twenty minutes later, Carla stood fuming at

the display of arrogance she could see in Shayne's quiet flirtation with their hostess.

What kind of a friend was Ms. Nicolette Daniels? Carla didn't much care, but she didn't like the woman making passes at her man.

Okay, she knew what she'd said about not being jealous, but Shayne was making it quite clear that he was testing her limits. And his arrogant smile at her didn't help to calm her already boiling temper.

Of course, "Cool Roger," as he called himself, wouldn't stop harassing her. As soon as Shayne had gone off to greet his hostess, this balding man had pounced on her. She ached to kick him in the nuts. If only he'd stop trying to sneak a feel of her bottom.

When she saw Shayne coming in her direction, she sighed in relief. She'd had enough. She couldn't take it anymore.

"So how are you enjoying yourself?"

She wanted to wipe the smirk from his face. "From what I can see, not as much as you are. Ms. Nicolette can't keep her hands off you."

"She can't? I didn't even realize." His tone was mocking.

"Realize, my ass. You're there slobbering all over her."

"Do I detect a hint of jealousy?"

At first, she didn't answer, but she couldn't give

him the satisfaction of believing that his silly attempt to make her jealous had any impact on her.

"Of course not," she finally said. "If that pathetic display of flirting is supposed to make me jealous, I assure you, you've failed."

'Oh, well, I just wondered. I just bade farewell to our hostess, so let's get on home."

"It's about time."

"I didn't know you wanted to leave. If I had known, we could have left earlier. However, I did enjoy the few times I danced and, since this is one of my favorite songs, I'm thinking that I should dance with the beautiful Carla Nevins before we leave."

Before she could refuse, he swept her into his arms and carried her onto the dance floor. She attempted to pull away.

"Will you please let us finish this dance? I've been aching to hold you all night, so behave yourself and enjoy what's left of the song."

Still fuming, but not wanting to make a fool of herself, Carla focused on the feel of the music. It was one of her favorite Whitney Houston songs so giving herself to the music was no problem.

There was no need to fight this moment. At least, there were people around, so he couldn't take advantage of her. Or so she thought.

Shayne pulled her closer until she could feel every contour of his firm hard body. When his hand came around her, she felt her body tremble. And then his hand started a leisurely caress of her back.

What was he trying to do to her?

Seduce her?

But he'd promised.

She wanted to say something to him, to stop him from working his magic on her.

She felt his body move against her to the rhythm of the bongo drums that pounded in her head. The music was within her and without. She could feel the pulse of each instrument flow through her veins and she felt alive.

It was only then that she realized that Whitney Houston no longer crooned, but that the sound of sweet calypso music beat in time with her heart.

Shayne still held her close, but the movement was faster, and then there were hands clapping and Carla joined in the revelry.

She saw another side of Shayne. The serious contemplative man became an African dancer, his body gyrating to the pounding beat. His hips moved in a seductive sway, sensually enticing her.

He was the seducer and she was the object of his seduction and he had every intention of winning. Then the music slowed to a hypnotic dance for lovers.

Carla could feel the heat of the inevitable, but knew that he was playing with her mind and feelings. She was sure now of what she wanted and, despite the slow seduction, she knew that resisting him was not about revenge, but about commitment.

That's why she had to do what she was doing. She did not want only a marriage. She wanted love.

And, as the lights dimmed, Carla closed her eyes and rested her head on Shayne's chest.

Chapter 13

Carla exited the car before Shayne could come around to open the door for her. She wanted to escape to her room. They'd danced until the party had ended, and every nerve in her body now tingled with awareness of the man she'd fallen hopelessly in love with.

She headed for the door, hoping to enter before he could join her, but stopped abruptly when she realized she didn't have a key. She had to wait for him.

She turned toward the car, watching as he locked it and came toward her.

"What's the hurry, Ms. Nevins? 'Fraid of the dark?" His voice was a whisper, soft and teasing.

She didn't answer. All she could think of was

how his body had felt against hers, the evidence of his arousal tantalizing her each time his body moved closer to her as they danced.

"Cat got your tongue? Then, I'm going to have to take care of that situation," he said.

With that, he pulled her toward him.

For a moment, they looked into each other's eyes, the awareness of what existed between them as clear as the moonlit night.

"Carla, I have no time to play this game of yours." He bent his head and captured her lips, wasting no time in parting them and exploring her sweetness.

Carla gave in to the inevitable, enjoying the thrill of his exploration.

When his lips left hers, she protested. She felt the zip at the back of her dress give way, giving him access to her exposed breasts.

She groaned, anticipating his mouth on her, her breasts already aching for his lips.

He pressed her against the wooden wall of the patio, among the trellises that climbed the walls.

She placed her hands on his head urging him on and the feeling of wholeness only made her hunger for more.

Shayne's head shifted, pleasuring the other breast, causing her to tremble with excitement.

He lifted her, taking her to one of the chairs in the shadows of the patio.

Before he sat, he pulled his pants down, exposing his throbbing penis, and the muscles of her vagina contracted involuntarily with excitement.

He sat, his shirt now unbuttoned, and reached for her. His hands slipped under her dress and pulled her panties down.

He spread his legs out, willing her to sit and she did. She moved onto his lap and guided his swollen thickness inside her.

His eyes were closed and the pleasure of his desire contorted his face, but somehow that excited her.

He wanted her and that knowledge thrilled her.

"Shayne, tell me how it feels. Talk to me."

And she moved on him with slow easy movements.

"Damn, Carla, this feels so good. I don't want it to stop. I love being inside you." He paused, his breath ragged.

She continued to move up and down, her hands finding his exposed nipples and rubbing them until he groaned.

"That feels so good. Don't stop. I don't want this to end. Love me. Love me."

And Carla loved it. She loved the excitement of it and she wanted to feel the thrill of the excitement. She increased her movements, wanting to bring him to that place of ultimate pleasure.

She moved faster, throwing her head back, and he joined her, his pelvis thrusting upward to meet each of her downward movements.

She felt that familiar pounding in her head and the rapid tensing of her muscles and she knew her climax was coming, and Shayne's words revealed his own impending release.

And then his body tensed, and she felt his penis contract and stiffen inside her and she heard his groans of pure unadulterated pleasure. She joined him with her own scream of passion, as spasm after spasm caused her to tremble against him.

Shayne held her tightly and the strangest thing happened, she saw the pools of water in his eyes.

Her man, her son's father, was crying.

She lowered her head toward him, kissing the tears away and he held her even tighter, as if he never wanted to let her go.

"Shayne, I love you," she whispered.

At first, she thought he'd not heard, but when he looked at her she saw her words reflected there.

There was no need for him to say anything, but he did.

"I love you, too. From the day I met you, I fell in love. I didn't know what it was, but that's all it could have been. I wasn't ready for it then, but it was love, all the same. I just needed time to admit that's what I was feeling."

"I know what you mean. I didn't want to fall in love again. When my husband and child died in that accident, I didn't want to feel that sense of loss again. But, unconsciously, I was falling in love with you and didn't want to admit it."

At her words, he kissed her, a deep, long kiss that left her aching all over for him.

In the distance, they heard the barking of a dog. "Maybe it's time we go on in. Wanna sleep with me tonight, Ms. Nevins?"

"Your wish is my command."

They took the time to make themselves presentable and then quietly entered the house. Shayne did not turn the lights on. When their eyes adjusted to the darkness, after kissing a few more times, they tiptoed upstairs, giggling when the floor creaked under their feet.

An hour later, after a long shower, Carla lay awake. Next to her Shayne was softly snoring. Tonight had not ended as she'd expected, but she was happy.

They'd talk in the morning. Shayne had promised.

Just before sunrise, Shayne stood at the window. He would ask her today. He wanted to marry her. He turned his eyes to her, feasting them on the woman who lay on his bed.

Even now, he wanted her, despite making love to her again in the wee hours of the morning.

He knew that he wanted to wake up each morning and find her in his bed. He wanted to see her stomach swollen again with his child, their child. Maybe a daughter the next time.

He wanted to marry her; he wanted her to carry the Knight family name.

He loved her.

Yes, he loved her. He'd never thought he could love someone like this.

True, there was lots he still needed to find out about her, facets of her personality he wanted to discover, but that would come in time.

In the distance, the sky was moving from black to a dark gray as the sun caressed the island with its first weak rays. As he watched, the gray, dawn sky turned in to the brilliant azure for which the Caribbean is known.

Shayne wanted to scream for joy, but he didn't want to wake Carla. She needed her rest.

Instead, he just stood there watching the sunrise and listened to the sound of the plantation as it came alive.

Just after sunrise, Carla woke to the pitter-patter of raindrops on the roof. She glanced at the space on the bed next to her and panicked.

He'd left again.

When she glanced around the room she saw him

standing at the window. He was naked and a familiar yearning stirred inside her. The sensation did not surprise her.

He was standing so still, she could almost imagine he was a stone statue, but Shayne was very much alive. His muscular buttocks beckoned her, and she remembered the feel of their firmness under her hands. Now, her hands ached to touch him.

He was lovely, and she felt the desire to capture him, just like that, standing at the window. She slipped from the bed and reached for her camera, snapping the picture before he noticed her.

"I hope I don't find that photo on the Internet sometime soon," he teased.

He opened his arms, welcoming her into the comfort of his warmth. She felt safe.

"Will you marry me, Carla?" he asked. "I want you to be my wife. I want to wake with you lying beside me each morning."

"I wondered when you were going to ask me properly."

"So, what's your answer?"

"Need I say? I love you, Shayne. Of course, I'll marry you."

"You've made me the happiest man in the world. We have to go let our son know today that his mommy and daddy are getting married."

"Of course we have to tell him first," she agreed.

"You're sure you're fine with this, Mrs. Knight-to-be?"

"Oh, very fine, Mr. Knight."

"Do you want me to show you how happy I am?"

"I do declare, I'd be delighted."

And Shayne set out to show her the total length of his happiness.

Gladys placed the last glass in the dishwasher and turned the power on.

She felt like jumping and skipping. They'd finally told her the good news. They were getting married.

She'd suspected something this morning when they'd come down for breakfast all lovey-dovey. Touching each other and sneaking feels under the table when she was serving them breakfast. *They must think I'm blind.*

But she didn't care. When they'd arrived from the hospital just a few minutes ago, they'd come to her in the sitting room and told her their news.

She'd lost control of her usual sense of decorum, had jumped up and squealed for joy, hugging both of them until Shayne had asked her if she intended to suffocate them.

Well, she was definitely going to have to buy that pink handbag to go with the dress that already hung in her wardrobe.

And shoes, too! She'd forgotten all about shoes. She'd have to go to Bridgetown this week. She didn't like the city crowd, but her favorite shoe shop was in the city. She was tired of asking them to open a branch nearby.

Epilogue

The day dawned perfectly for the wedding of the year in Barbados. Shayne stood by the window, his usual morning ritual. This morning everything seemed exceptionally beautiful. His senses seemed heightened, and the sky was clearer, the plantations sounds were music to his ears.

Suddenly, the morning became a musical symphony.

Russell, his brother, was at home for the summer and this morning the sweet melody of Russell's steelpan drum only served to make him feel even more ready for the day.

It had taken Carla and Gladys four months to

plan the wedding. That was just fine, because neither Shayne nor Carla wanted to get married until their son was able to attend the wedding. Though he'd been out of the hospital just over two months they hadn't wanted to expose him to a large crowd until Troy thought it was safe.

He turned and glanced at the bed. Last night was the first night in the past few months that Carla had not slept with him, but Gladys had insisted they do the proper thing.

According to her, they were already "fornicating," but she was all right with it because she knew they loved each other. But he was sure she'd be even happier when they were married and doing "it" legally and within the confines of her religious beliefs.

In a few hours, he'd be leaving the house to go over to George's where he, Russell and his best friends would be dressing for the wedding.

This wedding was going to be strange, but he'd insisted that he have two best men. He had no intention of making a choice between Troy and George. In fact, he wouldn't have wanted it any other way. Fortunately, the pastor at his church had agreed, so they were all set to walk up the aisle.

Slipping track pants on, he exited the room and headed to Carla's room. He wanted to see Darius before he left for George's home.

When he entered the room, his son was nursing. He bent to kiss Carla on the cheek.

"I'll be leaving shortly, Carla. Tamara and Gladys will help you dress for the wedding."

"I'm sure we'll be fine. Gladys is in charge, so everything has been planned to perfection. With Tamara and Sandra's help, I can't see anything going wrong," she said.

"Good, I can leave without worrying about anything."

"I'll see you later, honey. Love you."

"Love you, too," he replied, bending to kiss his son on the forehead. Darius gurgled and gave him a broad smile.

"'Bye, son, I expect you to be on your best behavior this afternoon."

As if he understood, Darius smiled sweetly.

"That's my boy. I'll see both of you later."

Downstairs, he found Russell and Tamara in the kitchen.

"'Morning, big brother," Russell greeted.

"Russell, Tamara. It's great to have both of you home. Remember, you have a home here for as long as you want. I'm sure you'll both marry eventually and move out."

"I don't even want to laugh," Tamara said. "And this from the man who vowed he'd never get married.

"Well, I am man enough to admit I was wrong. It took a wonderful woman to make me into an honest man."

"You did make a good choice. I like Carla. Knew she couldn't be half that bad when I heard she'd been reading my romance novels. Now that I've met her, I'm totally impressed. I didn't know my big brother had such good taste in women."

"Girl, I have good taste in most things. However, we have to be on our way, Russell. Hurry up and finish that cereal so we can go. George and Troy say they're making us breakfast."

He stopped to kiss Tamara. "Love you, sis."

"Love you, too. Don't worry. The wedding is going to be perfect."

"I know, sis. Everything is already perfect."

That night in the bridal suite of the Hilton Hotel, where they'd made love, Carla Nevins-Knight cuddled closer to her husband, her body radiant from their their lovemaking.

In a cradle nearby, their son, Darius, was fast asleep.

She was happy. Who would have thought that, in just one short year, her life would have changed so much? She was a mother and a wife and enjoying both of her roles. Their son had passed the worst times and was now a growing healthy boy.

"Carla, are you asleep?"

She opened her eyes. "No, just thinking," she replied.

"Thinking?"

"Yes, about all this. That so much has changed in the past year. I remember leaving to come to Barbados just to have fun. And here I am, a married woman and a mother."

"True, honey, so much has changed, but I know we've done the right thing. I want nothing more than to spend my life with you." Shayne smiled, hugged his new wife tightly, closed his eyes and was soon snoring softly.

Carla looked down at the man she loved more than life itself.

She smiled.

Paradise.

She was in paradise.

Gladys rocked her chair back and forth, her eyes focused on the moon above. All's well that ends well. She could rest for a while. But she wanted to see the others happy, too. Russell and Tamara would marry, but she hoped that George, Troy and Carla's best friend Sandra, found happiness, as well.

She wanted love for them just as she'd had it years ago. She'd lost her husband to cancer after twenty years of marriage, long before she'd come to work for the Knight family.

She smiled, remembering the wonderful times she'd had with him.

As the years passed, she'd never found someone else she could love as she'd loved him. And then Shayne, Russell and Tamara had needed her.

Today, she'd lost one of her children, but she was happy.

He'd found a good woman.

And, most importantly, the Knight heir was growing healthy and strong.

The wedding had been a beautiful one.

Carla had been lovely in a stunning gown made by one of the island's leading designers and Shayne had been so handsome in his black tuxedo that her heart had ached.

Of course, she'd created quite a stir in her pink dress!

Torn between her past and present...

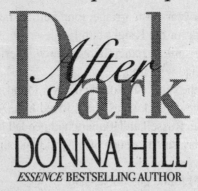

DONNA HILL

ESSENCE BESTSELLING AUTHOR

Elizabeth swore off men after her husband left her for
a younger woman...until sexy contractor Ron Powers
charmed his way into her life. But just as Elizabeth is
embarking on a journey of sensual self-discovery with
Ron, her ex tells her he wants her back. And with Ron's
radical past threatening their future, she's not sure what
to do! So she turns to her "girlz"—Stephanie, Barbara,
Anne Marie and Terri—for advice.

**Pause for Men: Five fabulously fortysomething divas
rewrite the book on romance.**

*Available the first week of July,
wherever books are sold.*

KIMANI™
ROMANCE

www.kimanipress.com

KPDH0240707

He's determined to become the
comeback kid...

THE VERY THOUGHT *of* YOU

ANGELA WEAVER

Drafted to hide a witness's daughter in a high-profile
murder case, Department of Justice operative
Miranda Tyler seeks the help of Caleb Blackfox,
who once betrayed her. Now Caleb is willing to do
whatever it takes to win back the girl who got away.

Available the first week of July,
wherever books are sold.

ESSENCE BESTSELLING AUTHOR

FRANCIS RAY

Undeniable

When Texas heiress Rachel Malone defied her powerful father to elope with Logan Prescott, Logan believed the marriage was forever. But that was before a trumped-up assault charge set the town and Rachel against him. With a heart full of pain, Logan left Stanton...and the bittersweet memories of the love he and Rachel shared. Now he's back, but is it for love or revenge?

> "Francis Ray creates characters and stories
> that we all love to read about."
> —*New York Times* bestselling author
> Eric Jerome Dickey

Available the first week of July wherever books are sold.

ARABESQUE®

www.kimanipress.com   KPFR0690707

Forgiveness takes courage...

A MEASURE OF
Faith

MAXINE BILLINGS

With her loving husband, a beautiful home and two
wonderful children, Lynnette Montgomery feels very
blessed. But a sudden car accident starts a chain of
events that tests her faith, and pulls to the forefront
memories of a very painful childhood. At forty years of
age, Lynnette comes to see that it takes a measure of
faith to help one through the pains of life.

"An enlightening read with an endearing family theme."
—Romantic Times BOOKreviews
on The Breaking Point

Available the first week of July
wherever books are sold.

Celebrating life every step of the way.

YOU ONLY GET *Better*

New York Times bestselling author

CONNIE BRISCOE

and

Essence bestselling authors

LOLITA FILES
ANITA BUNKLEY

Three fortysomething women discover that life, men and
everything else get better with age in this entertaining
three-in-one anthology from three award-winning authors!

Available the first week of March wherever books are sold.

KIMANI PRESS™
www.kimanipress.com